A BILLIONAIRE BUTLER for Christmas

dobi daniels

Luxhaven
Publishing

ISBN paperback, 978-1-958987-02-5

Interior Design by Luxhaven Publishing

Cover Design by The Book Brander Boutique

Editing by JD Book Services

Proofreading by Lisa Lee Proofreading

To JC, Grandma D, and DC, whom I love more than life itself.

Dexington Christmas Billionaires Series

A Billionaire Inventor for Christmas

Her Billionaire Butler for Christmas

Her Billionaire Dentist for Christmas

Dexington Doctor Billionaires Series

Loving The Billionaire Heir Doc

Loving The Billionaire Owner Doc

Loving The Billionaire Army Doc

Loving The Billionaire Boss Doc

Loving The Billionaire Cowboy Doc

A Cowboy Loves the Doctor Series

A Doctor Second Chance for the Rancher (prequel)

A Doctor Blind Date for the Cowboy

A Doctor Enemy for the Cowboy

A Doctor Billionaire for the Cowboy

Standalone

Her Billionaire Nemesis (short story)

SEE ALL OF DOBI DANIELS BOOKS

at https://dobidaniels.com.

AUTHOR'S NOTE

Thank you for choosing A BILLIONAIRE BUTLER FOR CHRISTMAS. I enjoyed writing the story of Emily Roth and Geoffrey Hart, a story of love and courage.

It's so easy to believe you are not worthy of true love after you've failed in love. I pray A BILLIONAIRE BUTLER FOR CHRISTMAS gives you the hope and courage to believe in yourself and love again.

Please continue this journey with me in A BILLIONAIRE DENTIST FOR CHRISTMAS, which is the follow-on story of Veronica, Sarah's friend, and how she found love. You can grab your copy at https://dobidaniels.com.

Would you like to be notified when the next Dobi Daniels book releases? Sign up at https://dobidaniels.com.

Once again, thank you so much for purchasing A BILLIONAIRE BUTLER FOR CHRISTMAS and for meeting Emily Roth and Geoffrey Hart. If you enjoyed it, please consider leaving a review at your favorite retailer or recommending it to a friend.

Thanks again for your support!

Dobi Daniels

A BILLIONAIRE BUTLER

for Christmas

CHAPTER 1

Emily Roth rubbed her ankles and winced. She'd only been standing a few hours, and they already hurt so much. She picked up one of her shoes and examined it. The heel was well-worn, and the shoe needed to be replaced, but Emily couldn't bear to part with it.

The shoes had been a gift from her mom before the disease claimed her mind. Emily was supposed to wear them for her first real job, but she'd gotten married instead after high school graduation, and that job had never materialized. Emily now wore them with the hope it would lead her to her first full-time job, which was supposed to happen in the next few weeks. In the meantime, she would resole the pair at the shoe cobbler's shop she'd discovered at the local strip mall. Money was tight, so she just needed a few more days till she was paid. "Don't let me down now," she muttered to the shoe.

"Are you okay?" a familiar voice asked. Emily looked up to see her colleague and friend, Nancy, lounging on a couch, which was oddly pink to match the light pink walls of the break room. She hadn't even noticed when she entered. Emily had known her since high school, and Nancy had been the one to invite her over to Dexington.

"Aren't you supposed to be on the floor?" Emily asked. They were both employees at a high-end boutique designer shop in the luxury Waterbridge Mall. Emily had joined five months ago, had worked hard taking care of the shop and its customers, and was due to be confirmed as a full-time employee any day now.

"I am," Nancy responded, swishing her smooth blonde ponytail. Sometimes, Emily wished her hair could be as cooperative. Nancy gave her an impish smile. "But I knew you would go on break soon, and I need a favor."

Emily slipped her shoes back on, got up from

the cushioned seat she'd been resting on, and lifted her wallet from her locker before shutting it. "What do you need?" This was the first time Nancy had asked her for anything.

"Could you grab me a cup of coffee?"

Emily's head spun so fast in Nancy's direction. "You are kidding, right? You know I can't bring coffee back here." The shop manager had drilled it into Emily's head on her first day that coffee or any other drink beyond water were not allowed in the boutique—it had to be consumed outside the shop.

Nancy let out a sigh. "Please? I wouldn't ask if I wasn't desperate. Perry had a rough night, and I can barely function on my feet." Perry was Nancy's son. He'd been in an accident a few weeks ago and had just been discharged home. He was slowly recovering but still had a rough time at night from nightmares of the accident. Emily had hoped the boy was doing better. "I can't even leave the shop now to grab one, or Tyrant would have my neck for leaving my post. It's already bad enough that I can't stop yawning." Tyrant was the nickname they'd given the shop manager. She was very strict and seemed to delight in giving Emily and Nancy a hard time.

Bringing the coffee in was risky, and Emily could lose her job over this. But Nancy had been there for Emily and welcomed her with open arms when she needed to get away from everything. She'd helped her find a job and an apartment and always had a listening ear whenever Emily needed it. Still it was a big risk.

"It's too dangerous. I could lose my job over this." And she needed this income till she graduated at the beginning of the New Year, by which time she would have the college degree she needed to apply for her dream job at Dexington Healthcare, the one place that didn't care about how much work experience she had at her age as long as she had a college degree. All the money she'd scrimped and saved in the past year after covering rent had gone into paying her remaining college tuition.

"I promise nothing is going to happen, and I even have a waterproof lunch bag you could put it in. No spills or accidents whatsoever. Pretty, please?"

"I don't—"

"Remember how I covered for you when you were running late last week?"

"But—"

"And I took an extra shift just so you could make your exams on time? Tyrant suspected something and found a reason to dock my pay, yet I never said a word. Please, Emily, I really need this."

Emily sighed. It was true she owed Nancy. Nancy had been the first to lend a hand during Emily's darkest moment—without her, Emily might not be where she was today. Nancy had done so without asking anything in return, and she really looked like she could barely stay on her feet despite the makeup she'd piled on to hide the bags under her eyes. "Okay, but you can't tell anyone."

Nancy ran over and gave her a quick hug. "Thank you."

"Don't thank me yet." Emily blew out an exhale. She'd only agreed because she'd overheard Tyrant saying she was going out to take care of some business.

Emily had planned to eat lunch at a coffee shop overlooking the park a few blocks away. But it was best to get this over with as soon as possible, so now it made more sense to grab a takeaway sandwich instead, along with the coffee, from the café across the street.

She would have to hurry before Tyrant returned, or else she could end up in a lot of trouble.

CHAPTER 2

"I'm sorry about this, sir," the valet said as he fidgeted under Geoffrey Hart's gaze.

Geoffrey sighed. It was common knowledge that the VIP reserved parking spot at the mall belonged exclusively to the Dexington family, yet someone had parked a boxy white Jetta in the space.

This was one of the reasons why he hated moving around during the Christmas season. Something weird always managed to happen to him during this time. He'd stopped liking Christmas after he lost his parents in different years during this same season that everyone always gushed about. His longtime girlfriend in college had dumped him and then subsequently died in an accident during this holiday too. He'd pretty much shut his heart to love after that, poured his energy into work, and tried his best to minimize his activities during this season. But he'd had no choice but to run this errand.

He checked the time on his Patek Philippe watch—he was running late and didn't have time to deal with this parking issue. He swept his eyes around the garage floor, but all the other spots were occupied.

"I'll take care of it, sir," the valet said with a solemn look on his face and extended his hand out to Geoffrey.

Geoffrey yielded the keys to his Range Rover SUV to him. He would have to trust the valet to handle it. He only had a little time to pick up the custom-ordered gift waiting for him at the boutique shop. It was an impromptu present ordered by his boss, Alex Dexington, for his wife, Helen, and had only just arrived a few hours ago.

Geoffrey, who worked as the family's butler, had planned to pick up the item later in the day, but Alex had called in the morning to inform him that they would be arriving from Europe in the afternoon, a week earlier than originally planned, and he hoped to present the gift to his wife today.

The house had been thrown into a bustle of activity as the staff got the house ready for their return, yet there was still so much to be done. Thank goodness this would be a quick get-in-get-out scenario.

Geoffrey glanced at the white Jetta one more time and then hurried toward the elevators that led into the mall.

CHAPTER 3

*E*mily peeked into the shop and caught a glimpse of Tyrant heading toward the rear of the boutique. *Shoot!* What was Tyrant doing back already when she was supposed to be out? Emily hadn't even wasted any time grabbing the coffee and her takeaway lunch, and had stashed both in the lunch bag she now carried.

Tyrant was the only one who could have the shop's closed sign hanging from the entrance and mainly for one reason only—there was a very important client she was attending to.

This wasn't good. How was Emily going to sneak the coffee in? There was no employee side door—all entrances and exits happened through the main sliding doors. The coffee was growing cold, Nancy was waiting, and Emily still had to eat lunch, and she couldn't wait till Tyrant was done with the client, since she had no idea when that would be. She'd seen client sessions range from fifteen minutes to two hours. Her break was going to be over soon, and Tyrant might dock her pay if she wasn't back on time.

She would have to go in silent as a mouse, especially since she had to bypass the client lounge area on her way to the break room. Hopefully, Tyrant would be occupied with the client and ignore her.

Emily stepped through the sliding doors into the shop. *Yikes!* Who had wiped the floor again? She'd cleaned it about an hour ago, and the next cleanup wasn't due anytime soon. She guessed Tyrant had insisted on it for this client.

Bad idea. What if the client tripped and fell? The marble floor had a tendency to do that in the first few minutes after it was cleaned. Good thing Emily had mastered walking on it.

Well she had to get going. Emily took a deep breath. She could do this. All she had to do was be careful.

What could possibly go wrong?

CHAPTER 4

"Here you go, Mr. Hart," the boutique shop manager said as she brought the garment bag to where Geoffrey sat waiting. The shop had been closed off temporarily for his use, a perk which he appreciated.

"Open it," Geoffrey requested.

The shop manager pulled up an empty clothes rack that was close by and hung the bag on it. Then she zipped down the bag, carefully extracted the pajamas set that lay within, and laid it on the sofa.

Geoffrey studied the sleepwear. Made of mulberry silk and Sea Island cotton with delicate handcrafted embroidery designs in Helen's favorite colors, it was exactly what Alex had ordered. He nodded in appreciation, and the shop manager picked up the set to place them back in the bag.

Then the unthinkable happened.

A scream rent the air, and Geoffrey looked in the direction of the sound only to see flailing hands and legs careening toward him. He watched in horror as a lunch bag flew into the air and hit the edge of the clothes rack, which ripped the bag, splattering dark brown liquid with a strong coffee smell all over the pajamas.

He stiffened and swung his eyes to see who the culprit was, the person that had unleashed this mayhem. But a sharp indescribable pain hit his core at that moment.

Geoffrey gasped, and his knees buckled and hit the floor. With the most intense pain he'd ever experienced shooting through his body, he looked down only to see a foot—encased in a high heeled shoe—against his groin.

"Are you okay?" Geoffrey could hear the shop manager's voice as if in a distance, but he focused on taking deep breaths to bring the pain in his groin under control.

"I'm so sorry, I'm so sorry," another female voice said, which he guessed belonged to the culprit. He felt hands grabbing his arms as a soft gardenia scent filled his nostrils.

"Don't touch me!" Geoffrey croaked out as he waved the hands away. He gritted his teeth against the pain and forced himself back onto the sofa. What had she been thinking? He'd shopped here enough times to be sure coffee was not allowed in the shop. His eyes swung to where the pajamas now lay, ruined. What was he going to do?

"I'm so sorry," the female voice repeated.

Geoffrey ignored her and ran his hand through his hair. He didn't need her apology—that wasn't going to solve anything. They needed a solution to remedy the situation. There was no way he could tell Mr. Dexington that his gift had been damaged.

"My apologies, Mr. Hart. I'm so sorry about all of this," the shop manager said in a contrite tone. "Go," she commanded to the person he'd guessed was the culprit.

Geoffrey looked up to see the back profile of a petite lady with her blonde hair swept up in a loose chignon, revealing a graceful neck, and wearing a coffee-streaked white blouse, walking away with her shoulders hunched. Something about her struck a chord within him, and he wanted to ask her if she was okay. But he held back. What had happened was all her fault, and he still needed to fix the damaged sleepwear.

He turned to the shop manager. "Is there another set?" he asked. Though dry cleaning could work wonders on the stained outfit, this item was supposed to be a gift. So it was up to the shop to take care of the mistake.

"Let me call Miss James and find out," the shop manager said and hurried off. Miss James was the designer and owner of the shop.

Geoffrey looked down at himself. There were a few brown streaks on his otherwise pristine white shirt and darker stains on his grey pants, but nothing he couldn't make do with till he got home.

Soon the manager returned. "Miss James has another pair in a slightly different color but in the same color scheme, and it's still at her design studio in Atlanta," she said. "She'll need to make a few modifications and can send it out in the next two hours, but it won't get here until tomorrow."

That wouldn't work. Mr. Dexington had to get the item today. "I need it tonight at the latest," Geoffrey said. "I can have our pilot head out to the studio immediately to pick it up." It would take about two-and-a-half hours from Dexington to reach Atlanta.

"That should work. I'll let Miss James know and get the address for you." The manager rushed off to make the arrangements, while another shop attendant cleaned up the mess on the floor.

Geoffrey pulled out his phone and made a quick call to the pilot to place him on standby. The sharp pain in his groin had died down, leaving a dull ache in its place. Geoffrey guessed it would be a few hours till the pain was completely gone. He looked around to see if he could spot the blonde that had caused the mayhem, but she was nowhere in sight.

The manager soon returned. "Here you go, Mr. Hart," she said as she extended a sheet of paper to him. "Miss James is very sorry about what happened and will be refunding half of the cost."

"That won't be necessary," Geoffrey said.

"She insists, Mr. Hart."

"Okay." If that was what she wanted. His mind had already moved on to the one-million-

and-one things he needed to take care of, and he had yet to update the pilot.

Geoffrey got up and speed-dialed the pilot's number as he headed out of the shop.

But his mind flickered back to the woman who had caused the incident.

He hoped she wouldn't be disciplined too harshly.

CHAPTER 5

"Miss Roth, you've caused a lot of trouble today," Tyrant said as Emily stood before her in the tiny beige-colored cubicle that served as her office. Tyrant sat in a swivel chair behind her desk, which was filled on one side with stacks of paper arranged in neat rows.

"I'm sorry. I didn't mean—"

"We have those rules in place for a reason, yet you chose to break it. As a result, the shop lost a lot of money, and you hurt a very important customer. What if he decides to close the account with the shop because of this, or word-of-mouth rumor spreads about how we don't take good care of our clients and products?"

Emily kept silent. There was nothing she could say to that. The rules were clear, and she just hoped breaking one had not cost her too much.

Tyrant removed her glasses, placed them on her desk, and sighed. Then, in a quieter tone, she said, "Emily, we can't keep you on even if we want. I doubt the customer would like that, and we need to keep him happy." She put her glasses back on, picked up a white envelope, and slid it toward Emily. "Miss Roth, you are fired. Here's your last paycheck. Please clear out your locker in the next twenty minutes."

Emily's heart sank. She'd expected to be punished, but she'd hoped it wouldn't be this. How was she going to manage financially till the New Year? Good jobs weren't exactly easy to find, and her rent was due soon. The last thing she needed was to be thrown out into the streets, and during Christmas season no less. Luckily, she still had some time before she had to make her final tuition payment, so that could wait.

"Good day, Miss Roth," the shop manager said in a dismissive tone and turned to the paperwork on her desk.

It was all her fault. She'd known the rules,

and yet had let her emotions override her sense of caution. And now it had cost her. How was she going to pay her bills? This job was supposed to be her safety net while she hunted for a new job after she graduated. How could she have been so foolish?

Emily halted. But Tyrant had mentioned they might have kept her on the job if not to please the handsome customer. Yes, she'd noticed the lean build that filled out his crisp white shirt, and his beautiful brown eyes that looked like pools of yummy chocolate, the type she could never get tired off.

The jerk. She'd done wrong, but his outburst had probably tipped the scale on getting her fired, even though she'd been a model employee and had been praised numerous times by other customers.

And why had he treated her like she was some sort of leper when she'd tried to help him up? Being poor didn't mean she was dirty. She'd only been trying to rectify her mistake.

Her shoulders fell. It was no use thinking about it now. She needed to figure out what to do next.

Emily resumed walking and soon entered the break room and headed to her locker. She opened it and began to put her belongings into the gym bag she always left there.

"I'm sorry," Nancy whispered beside her. Emily hadn't heard her approach.

She kept silent and continued removing her things from the locker.

"Emily ..."

Emily turned and faced her. She could see the unshed tears in Nancy's blue eyes.

She let out a sigh. There was no way she could stay mad at her friend, and it had been Emily's choice at the end. "It's all done. There's nothing either of us can do about it now," she said.

"I'm going to tell Tyrant it was me. That it was all my fault," Nancy said. She brushed past Emily and moved toward the door.

Emily grabbed her arm. "Don't go. It's no use. I can't have you fired too. You need the money to take care of Perry."

Nancy's arm dropped to her side. "I'm sorry."

"Don't be. Besides, who says I won't get a

better job?" She patted her friend's shoulder and then turned back to her locker.

"But how are you going to make rent?"

"I'll figure something out."

"You could move in with us, you know."

Emily gave Nancy a small smile. She appreciated the offer, but Nancy's place was already tight with her, Perry, and her parents living in the same apartment. Emily preferred her own space.

The door opened, and another employee poked her head in. "Nancy, you are needed on the floor," she said.

"I have to go," Nancy said to Emily. "I'll call you later, okay?"

Emily nodded and kept her eyes on her locker till Nancy left and shut the door behind her. Then she collapsed against the locker and fought back the tears that threatened to fill her eyes. What was she going to do now?

She took a deep breath and exhaled. This was not the time or place to break down. She had to finish up here and find a job. Emily turned back to the locker and continued packing till it was empty, and then she closed the locker a final time.

She could find another job. Easier said than done but not impossible. Thank goodness she'd finished all her exams earlier this week—she couldn't imagine studying and dealing with this at the same time. She just needed to find a paying job, figure out a way to make her rent, and hang in there for the next couple of weeks till she could apply to Dexington Healthcare. She'd spent a long time studying about the company and was optimistic about her chances at applying there.

She only had to survive till then.

Emily squared her shoulders, picked up her gym bag, and headed out.

Emily looked around the parking lot, filled with an assortment of mostly luxury vehicles. Where was her car? She was pretty sure she had parked it here, in the spot in front of her.

She'd been running late when she arrived this morning, and the parking spot had been empty, like it was most times, so she'd taken the chance to use the space. Her colleagues did it too when they were in a hurry, with the valet service turning a blind eye. It was a running joke that the owners of the spot were probably dead since no one ever really parked there. So why was her car missing from the spot?

A sense of dread filled Emily. It couldn't be, right? No, it wasn't possible. There was no way the owner would show up today of all days. It had to be another reason, and the valet folks would probably know.

Emily headed over to the valet booth on the same floor. A young girl in her twenties with freckles all over her nose looked up as she approached. Emily had seen her around but couldn't remember her name. "Hi, have you seen a white car parked in the VIP lot near the elevators?"

"A boxy-looking Jetta?" the girl asked.

Emily's heart accelerated. "Yes."

"It was towed about thirty minutes ago. You have to go down to this address and pick it up," she said and handed Emily a card.

It was just her luck to get caught the one time she'd decided to take advantage of the spot. This day couldn't get any worse. "Why?"

"The owner of the spot came today. Tim had to apologize to him over and over again." Tim was the valet-in-charge of this parking floor. "Nice-looking man too. Beautiful eyes."

Emily's heart quickened. Could it be the same guy? "Do you remember what he was wearing?"

"You mean the customer?" Emily nodded. The girl scrunched up her face as if in thought. "I believe it was a white shirt with rolled up sleeves and grey pants."

Emily froze. She was pretty sure it was the same guy. She'd lost her job and her car had been towed because of him. How could one person bring such bad luck to her?

"Thank you," Emily said to the girl and turned away.

She slung her gym bag over her shoulder and headed toward the exit. First, she needed to get her car back, even if it was going to make her about two-hundred-dollars poorer.

Emily winced. That was money she couldn't afford to lose now, but she had no choice. She would deposit her last paycheck at an ATM on her way to the tow yard to cover the cost, but paying for the expense might put her account in the red.

Her shoulders fell. She really needed a job like yesterday if she wanted to make her rent.

Emily's phone buzzed, and she pulled it out and looked at the screen. It was a text message from Nancy.

Nancy: I just heard there's a marketing assistant opening at the Holly Hoo Christmas tree farm. They are looking to fill it urgently, and they pay well. It might be worth a look.

Emily grimaced. She was not a fan of all things Christmas because of what happened in the past. She could handle the season for a short period, but working at the farm would mean being exposed to it all the time, something she was not comfortable with, even though the job sounded interesting. But beggars could not be choosers, and she had to consider it since she needed the money. Nothing said she had to work there longer than a few months.

She typed out a response.

Emily: Thank you.

Nancy: It's the least I can do to make up for everything. I'll let you know if I hear anything else.

Emily: Okay.

Nancy: Talk to you later.

Emily replaced the phone back in her pocket. She had nothing to lose from applying, and she needed to do it soon. Maybe the job would turn out to be the miracle she needed.

But first she had to go pick up her car.

CHAPTER 6

The doorbell jingled as Geoffrey entered the dry-cleaning establishment after his morning run. He'd been using the small oddly-shaped shop since forever and had seen no reason to discontinue even after he gained his own property on the vast Dexington estate. If anything, he was a creature of habit.

The Dexingtons had returned yesterday, and Helen had been over the moon at Alex's gift. It had been worth the stress to ensure its arrival on time. Since he had the morning off, Geoffrey figured it was a good time as any to pick up his laundry before heading off to attend to the Christmas farm, one of his investments.

He strode to the counter and noticed a lady

he didn't recognize sitting behind it and reading a book. Rows of clothes in transparent garment bags hung on wall racks behind her. "Hello," he said. "I'm here to pick up my laundry."

Pale blue eyes stared up at him and then widened. "You!" she said. She looked at him up and down. "I almost didn't recognize you in your outfit."

What did that mean? Geoffrey studied her. He couldn't recall ever seeing her before. "Do you know me?" he asked.

"Aren't you the man from the boutique shop? The one who got my friend fired? Fancy meeting you here," she said as her eyes hardened.

What was she talking about? Which friend?

She must have sensed his confusion because she continued. "The shop where coffee got spilled on you."

The memories of yesterday's incident came rushing back. Oh, that boutique shop! Was her friend the blonde who had caused the accident? Sure, she had wronged him, but he hadn't expected she would lose her job. "She got fired?"

"I see you now remember," the woman said.

"Yes, she got fired. I know she did wrong, but isn't it extreme that she had to lose her job because of it? And just when she was doing so well. Now the poor girl may not even be able to make her rent and might end up on the streets with no roof over her head. Because of you," she said pointedly.

Geoffrey shifted from one foot to the other. Now he was feeling bad about what happened. The last thing he ever wanted was to make anybody's life harder. "Where is she?" he asked.

"Why?" The woman peered at him with curiosity-filled eyes. "Do you want to get her fired again?"

"No, I'd like to apologize."

The woman studied him for a moment. "What's the name on the laundry?" she asked.

So she didn't want to tell him. Maybe she didn't trust him, which was normal given that they were practically strangers. Geoffrey decided to let the subject drop. He would have to find another way to track the blonde down. "Geoffrey Hart," he responded.

The woman headed into the back room and soon returned with his items. He noticed her demeanor had changed. What had happened back there?

She placed his clothes on the counter. "Are you the same Geoffrey that has been coming to this shop for years?"

"Most likely," Geoffrey said. "Why do you ask?"

Her face relaxed. "So, you're the one my parents are always talking about! Your clothes have the silver tag that my parents reserve for long-time customers."

So she was the owners' daughter. No wonder she felt very comfortable speaking to him this way. She obviously wasn't worried what the owners would say if they heard about it. But how had she known about the coffee incident?

"I work at the boutique shop," she answered as if reading his mind. "I'm only here to cover for my parents since I have the day off."

Geoffrey picked up his clothes, paid the bill, and turned to leave.

"Her name is Emily Roth," the woman said. "Here's her number."

Geoffrey turned to see she'd slid a sheet of paper across the counter. He picked it up and stuffed it into his pocket. "Thanks," he said.

Then he swung the door open and stepped outside. The morning air was still slightly chilly, but the temperatures would grow warmer once the sun came out shortly.

Geoffrey pulled out the piece of paper from his pocket.

Emily Roth. A beautiful name. He wasn't sure if it was really a good idea to call her, yet his conscience wouldn't let him just gloss over it.

He returned the paper to his pocket. He would call her later today once he was done with his appointments.

But now he needed to get home, shower, change, and head over to the Christmas farm.

CHAPTER 7

Emily flipped through a magazine she'd found on the coffee table as she waited in the lobby of the Christmas farm's administrative building. She had applied for the job as soon as she got home after picking up her car and had been pleasantly surprised to receive an email interview notice for today a few hours later.

She'd expected a tiny business operation but had been surprised to enter a large farm filled with acres and acres of Christmas trees with a large administrative building at the center of it all. The building's lobby was designed in a mix of pleasing modern and Christmas themes without being gaudy, and a faint pine scent filled the air. The whole place looked warm and inviting. Emily hoped she would get the job.

A sudden urge hit her lower abdomen. *Ouch!* This was the wrongest time to need to use the bathroom. She was the first one scheduled to go in for the interview, so chances were slim there would be any delays.

Emily looked at her watch. She had twenty minutes to make a quick run to the bathroom and back, less if they called her in early. But she had to take the chance—she could make it if she hurried. It was better than wriggling in discomfort from a full bladder during the interview.

She rose to her feet and strode over to where the receptionist was busy typing on his computer. The young man looked up as Emily approached and gave her a warm smile. "How may I help you?" he asked.

"I'd like to use the bathroom," Emily said.

"Go through this doorway," he said, pointing to a set of French double doors on the right. "It's the third door on your left." He swiped a badge on the reader on the desk, and Emily heard a clicking sound emanating from the French doors.

"Thank you," she said.

She hurried through the double doors, her black high heels *click-clacking* on the cream- and black-speckled terrazzo floor. A yellow spin mop was propped in its bucket against the wall outside the bathroom door, but Emily ignored it and pushed her way in.

A few minutes later, she was done. She stepped out of the bathroom, smoothing down the light grey A-line dress she'd worn for the interview. She checked her watch to see how much time she had left.

A solid body hit her, and Emily found herself hurtling toward the ground, her leg knocking down the spin mop. The bucket turned over, and dark-colored water spilled from it, splattering large drops on Emily's dress. She watched in horror as dark stains covered the lower half of her dress.

Emily's head jerked up to see who had caused her misfortune, and her eyes widened.

How was it possible?

CHAPTER 8

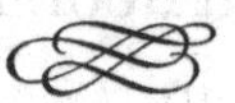

Geoffrey hurried through the French double doors as the receptionist buzzed him in. He was later than he preferred and was sure Steve Henshaw—the owner of the Holly Hoo Christmas farm—was already getting antsy at his non-appearance, since the interviews were scheduled to start soon.

Geoffrey had bought twenty-five percent of the farm a couple of years ago when it had run into financial troubles. The business had bounced back into the black the following year and now earned a healthy return on an annual basis.

Even though it seemed late in the game to do

so, hiring a new marketing assistant who could bring fresh ideas to the farm was one of the moves Geoffrey believed would further help increase sales this season. Steve typically had complete control over all HR decisions per their agreement, but he had requested Geoffrey's help for this interview, and Geoffrey had accepted. Between the two of them, they would make sure the right person was hired.

He glanced at his watch as he made his way down the hallway toward the conference room where the interviews would take place. He only had a few minutes left to discuss the applicants with Steve before they started the interviews.

Something solid bumped into his side, and pain shot through his hip. Geoffrey staggered and frowned at the offending party. But his look turned into one of intrigue at the blonde bombshell who had ended up on the floor and was now trying to wipe away the stains on her dress. Something about her looked familiar, but Geoffrey couldn't place who she was. Maybe he'd seen her before on one of his previous visits to the farm.

"Are you okay?" Geoffrey asked, extending a hand to her.

She looked up with beautiful brown eyes that widened and then shot darts of anger at him. But the lady said nothing and just took his proffered hand.

Geoffrey couldn't help the smile that tugged at the corners of his lips. This one was definitely a spitfire.

He felt a zap of electricity buzz through his skin as their hands touched. She must have felt it too, because she withdrew her hand immediately once she was on her feet. But her dress was now a mess. The stains looked like a mad man's attempt at polka dot design.

"I'm sorry," Geoffrey said. "Are you alright?"

"You should watch where you're going," she said in a frigid tone.

Hold on! What was with her? It wasn't like he deliberately ran into her, and she probably hadn't paid attention to where she was going as well. Two wrongs didn't make a right, but something about the tone of her voice irked him in that moment, and he couldn't help responding. "You weren't concentrating either," he pointed out.

She glared at him, a look that would have

frozen him on the spot if that was possible. "I can't even …" She pivoted and rushed back into the bathroom.

Geoffrey ran a hand through his hair. This wasn't like him to respond in such a childish manner. Her dress was ruined, and he should have focused on a solution that would take care of it. He thought about waiting for her till she was done, but it would most likely make things worse.

A soft scent of gardenias tickled his nose from where she'd stood. He knew this scent, but from where? Her back profile with the lovely blonde hair also seemed strangely familiar, but he still couldn't place where he had seen her before.

His phone buzzed, and Geoffrey pulled it out from his jacket and looked at the screen. It was Steve, probably calling to find out where he was. *Shoot!* He'd totally forgotten he had somewhere to be.

Geoffrey glanced at the bathroom door. He hoped she was able to get rid of all the stains.

Then he turned and hastened off in the direction of the conference room.

Emily brushed down the front of her dress one final time and examined herself in the full-length mirror on the restroom wall. She still looked somewhat presentable after managing to remove most of the stains, though a few still remained. But one would have to look closely to find them.

Her shoulders relaxed, and she let out a sigh of relief. Thank goodness there was still hope. It would have been totally unprofessional to show up for an interview in a dirty dress. First impressions really did matter, especially since she needed this job.

Emily froze. But what was that man doing here? She couldn't believe she'd crashed into him again. She'd been annoyed at seeing him, yet she couldn't deny that he looked gorgeous in his well-tailored suit topped with a red pocket square—Emily had always had a preference for matured men—and she'd felt a spark when his hand held hers.

But that didn't mean anything or change the fact that she disliked him. She'd ended up on the floor both times they'd met. This man was definitely someone to be avoided.

Emily quickly brushed down the tendrils of her hair that had escaped from its ponytail. But who was he, and why was he at the farm? Maybe he was an employee here. No, that wasn't possible. The boutique where she used to work catered exclusively to the nouveau rich—there was no way a mere employee could afford the shop's items.

Her hand stilled, and she gasped. Was he the owner of the farm? *Please let it not be true.* Because that would really be disastrous. Getting the job in that case would be a lost cause.

But wait! Emily had seen a picture in the lobby that showed the farm's executives, and the man was not one of them. Maybe he was just visiting someone at the farm. Yes, that was it, because any other possibilities were unfathomable.

She glanced at her watch, and her heart rate increased. She only had two minutes left to head back to the lobby! This was why this man was dangerous for her—just thinking about him had made her lose track of time! She had to hurry, or she might lose this chance.

Emily flew out the bathroom door and down the hallway to the reception. She pushed through the double doors just in time to hear her name being called.

A smartly-dressed woman with a pixie cut checked off Emily's name on the clipboard she held, led her back through the hallway Emily had just come through till they arrived at a door to what looked like a conference room. The woman knocked on the door, opened it, and then gestured for Emily to go in.

Emily straightened her shoulders. This was it. Time to do everything to make sure she bagged the job. She pasted a smile on her face and strode into the room with as much confidence as she could muster.

The conference room was smaller than she'd expected. There was a small round table in the center with three chairs around it. Two men were already seated at the table and were flipping through some documents in front of them.

Then the man on the right looked up.

Emily's heart dropped to the floor.

Emily fought to maintain her composure. It hadn't even occurred to her he might be her interviewer! *Relax, Emily. You can do this.*

She kept her face serene and managed to smile at them as she approached the table. "Good morning," she said, avoiding any direct eye contact with the man.

A dark-haired man with a salt and pepper goatee stood up and extended his hand to her across the table. "Welcome to Holly Hoo Farm, Miss Roth." Emily noticed the other man froze for a moment but then continued arranging the papers in front of him. "I'm Steve Henshaw, and I'm the owner of the farm. And this is my colleague, Geoffrey Hart," he said.

Emily shook Steve's hand in return. So that was the man's name. Geoffrey Hart. It sounded rather stuffy and seemed to suit him. Mr. Hart gave her a nod and said nothing else.

Really? That's it?

"Please sit," Steve said and gestured at the available seat.

"Thank you," Emily said and sat down. Time to focus on what she'd come here for, which meant ignoring Mr. Hart and putting her best foot forward.

"So Miss Roth, are you a native of Dexington?" Steve asked.

"No, I'm from New Jersey. I moved to Dexington early this year."

"Really? You don't have the accent."

Emily chuckled. "Not everyone from New Jersey does."

"Why did you move?" The question was from Mr. Hart.

Emily forced herself to maintain a steady gaze with him. "To explore better opportunities."

"Interesting, considering that New Jersey has a lot of job prospects," Mr. Hart countered. He leaned forward, his eyes boring into hers.

Emily's body tensed. Was he calling her a liar? How dare he when he knew nothing about her life! But she couldn't mess up this interview no matter what.

She steadied her breath and gave him a sweet smile. "But Dexington has a strong welcoming community and is a great place to put down roots." *Take that, you egotistical maniac.*

Steve nodded appreciatively. "It definitely is. Do you have family here?"

"I have good friends here."

"Great."

Emily relaxed. Bullet dodged. She had been afraid that they would probe into the real reason why she left New Jersey. Her past needed to stay buried.

Steve looked down at the sheet in front of him and then looked up. "Do you know how to use a chainsaw?"

Hold on one second. Where was that coming from? Was this one of those weird interviews she'd only heard about where they ask random questions that have nothing to do with the job in question? She was supposed to be applying for a marketing position if she remembered correctly. What did that have to do with a chainsaw? Well, she would tell them the truth.

"No, I've never used one. But I could learn how to if needed."

Steve nodded as if satisfied with her answer.

The rest of the interview flew by. Steve asked a lot of questions about her background and experience. Then he posed marketing case questions and listened to how she would solve them. The conversation was fun and somewhat light-hearted, unlike what she had expected. Mr. Hart said nothing throughout the process and just appeared to be listening, but she could feel his eyes on her anytime he raised his head.

Soon, the conversation started winding down, and Emily couldn't wait for it to end. Even though the interview seemed to have gone well so far, she feared that might change if the interview went on any longer.

"I'm afraid that's all the questions I have," Steve said. "Geoffrey, do you have any other questions for Miss Roth?"

Mr. Hart set down the paper he had been examining and leaned back.

Emily's heart raced. *Please don't mess this up for me,* she pleaded silently.

"Miss Roth, why do you need this job?"

She exhaled quietly. That was easy enough.

"I believe experiencing the magic of Christmas isn't complete without having a really good Christmas tree, and I would love to help more customers experience how special it is to own one, which would help the farm make more Christmas sales."

Mr. Hart gave her a look of disbelief. "Really?"

What did he mean by that? The tension in the room rose as Mr. Hart stared at her and said nothing. Did he always have to make things difficult for her? It wasn't as if she was owing him some huge debt. He looked at her like if he could see right through her and knew about her situation. *Wait!* Did he really know about what had happened to her?

Panic rose within Emily as she stared back at him. He knew, he really knew! Had he gone back to the shop to make sure she'd been fired? How else would he have known?

Soon anger replaced her anxiety. Even if he knew, did he have to make her say it? Well, if he wanted the truth, that was exactly what he was going to get.

"I also need the job urgently to pay my rent."

There. That was what he had wanted to hear,

wasn't it? She was not ashamed of her reason. There was nothing wrong with seeking honest labor to meet her basic needs. But she might have potentially tanked an otherwise great interview with her answer.

Steve cleared his throat. "Thank you so much for being honest with us, Miss Roth." He stood up and extended his hand to her. "It was great meeting you. We'll let you know within the next twenty-four hours what our decision is."

Emily shook his hand. "Thank you for the opportunity," she said.

The interview was over, just like that. She didn't know if she had passed or failed. But it was what it was. Right now, all she could do was hold her head up high and leave with confidence.

And that was exactly what Emily did as she picked up her things and left the room.

CHAPTER 10

"Chainsaw? Really?" Geoffrey said with a raised brow at Steve.

Steve shrugged. "Hey, I had to ask," he said. "This is a Christmas farm after all, and she might need to help cut down a Christmas tree in an emergency situation."

"I'm pretty sure it would never come to that."

"You never know. Come to think of it, did you have to poke her like that?"

"What do you mean?"

"Don't pretend. I saw what you did at the end."

Geoffrey leaned back. "We need someone who is not afraid to tell us like it is and won't cower. You can be pretty intimidating with that facial bush of yours."

Steve rubbed his jaw. "I'll have you know this fine goatee brings me good luck." He leaned forward. "But why do I sense there was something else behind that question?"

Geoffrey had no idea why he'd done it. It had been a spontaneous question. Maybe he'd wanted to see a glimpse of the real Emily Roth, not the persona she brought to the interview. He'd been shocked to see her enter the room and was even more surprised when Steve had mentioned her name. The memory of who she was had clicked into place.

"You don't know what you're talking about," Geoffrey said. "So, what do you think about her?"

Steve straightened. "I think she was great. She certainly knew her stuff and had some really cool ideas that could make a difference. Just what we were looking for. But she has no college degree."

"I don't remember that being a requirement, and she seems to be graduating soon."

"Isn't she too old to be graduating from college right now? She doesn't have a lot of working experience, which would have accounted for the delay. So what has she been doing for the past few years?"

"I thought she had some working experience in that time."

"But it was mostly volunteer work. Why wasn't it a paying job?"

"Why didn't you ask her?" Geoffrey said.

"Because I noticed you staring at her with star-struck eyes."

Geoffrey's face grew hot. "I was not!"

"You like her, don't you?"

"Hey, be careful. Someone hearing you say that would call this sexual harassment in the workplace." Geoffrey crossed his arms over his chest. "All I'm doing is being fair in her assessment."

"You know what I mean. You are usually cautious and like to follow protocol. Yet here you are defending her." Steve peered at Geoffrey curiously. "Hmmm ... it almost seems like you've met each other before."

Geoffrey sighed. Steve was like a dog with a bone if he sensed something. It was less troublesome for Geoffrey to just tell him. "I found out this morning I might be the reason she's looking for a new job."

Steve sat up. "What happened?"

There was no way he was telling Steve about the kick to the groin. The teasing would never end if he did. "The details don't matter. I just feel a bit guilty about it."

"So you want her to get the job."

"I didn't say that. It's more important if she's a good fit for it."

Steve laughed. "You can't fool me. You have a thing for her." He slapped Geoffrey's back. "It's about time, old man. You aren't getting younger. I've been worried about you not even showing interest in anyone over these years."

"That's not it!"

"Keep telling yourself that. You can't deny she's a pretty damsel in distress. Coupled with the brains, she is a powerful combination." Steve leaned back. "Anyway, we'll finish up the other interviews for today. In the meantime, I'll have HR look into her and make sure everything checks out, and we'll take your recommendation into advisement. If it doesn't work out, I'll make a few calls on her behalf. Either way, we'll make sure you're good, old man."

"Thanks."

"No problem."

Geoffrey relaxed. He hoped Miss Roth would get the job.

Then he could finally ditch the new guilt from this morning that weighed down his shoulders.

CHAPTER 11

*E*mily stepped into the small space that was her apartment and shut the door behind her. A tiny cream-colored one-bedroom suite pre-furnished and decorated with pops of teal and burnt orange, it was her very own place to call home, something she hadn't really had for a long time. This was the place that witnessed her many nights of tears, then peace, and finally hope.

She removed her heels, dropped her car keys into a small teal tray nestled at a corner of the tiny kitchen counter, and walked over to the lone couch in the living room space, falling into it.

Emily was bone tired. It was as if the effects

of what had happened in the last twenty-four hours were only now catching up with her. And the memory of today's interview was not helping.

She'd thought she had a fair shot at the job with the way the interview was going, but Mr. Hart had rained on her parade. How could he have been there of all places to mess up everything? Now her morning—time she would have used to job-hunt—had literally been wasted, and she still needed to find a way to pay her bills. Even though the Christmas farm job wouldn't have paid her immediately, it would have given her the confidence to borrow money from Nancy, knowing she could pay her back soon.

Emily rubbed at her temples to ease away the headache that lurked. Maybe her only choice at this point was to find an hourly wage job that would help her take care of her urgent bills first. Then she would have enough time to find a more secure option.

Her phone buzzed in her bag beside her, and Emily pulled it out and looked at the screen. It was Nancy. "Hello, Nancy," she said after swiping the answer button.

"Hey. How did it go?"

Emily let out a long sigh. "I don't think I got the job."

"What do you mean? Any employer would be lucky to hire you."

"I met Mr. Unlucky there."

"Who?"

"The guy I ran into at the boutique."

"You mean the one you kicked in the groin?"

"You don't have to remind me. Yes, him."

"Sorry," Nancy said. "You met him at the Christmas farm? Did he come to buy a tree?"

"I wish. He was one of my interviewers."

"Ouch."

"Ouch indeed. First, I bumped into him coming out of the bathroom and landed flat on my face, which wasn't the best first impression, and then he ended up as my interviewer. Talk about a bad day."

"I hope it wasn't because of what I said to him earlier."

"What do you mean?"

"I met him this morning at my parents' dry cleaning place, and I gave him a piece of my mind about what happened to you."

Emily groaned. "I'm screwed."

"I'm sorry. I had no idea he would be at the

farm. But, Emily, are you sure there isn't something bound to happen between you two?"

Emily sat up. "How can you say that?"

"I don't know. There has to be a reason why you guys keep bumping into each other."

"I doubt it."

"You don't think he's cute?"

"I wouldn't use the word 'cute', maybe ...."

"Handsome?" Nancy chuckled. "See? You noticed."

It wasn't like she was blind. Mr. Hart wasn't as tall as her ex, but his height was perfect for her petite frame. Not that she was thinking she would go out with him or anything—there was no way oil and water could mix.

Emily scoffed. "Don't worry. Nothing is *ever* going to happen."

Nancy laughed. "If you say so. Did they mention when they would get back to you about the job?"

"In the next twenty-four hours."

"So there's still hope."

"Maybe, but I'm not betting my money on it. I need to keep looking."

"Don't worry. You'll find a good one soon. I'll keep my ears open for any news."

"Thanks."

A loud knock sounded on the door, and Emily's head swung in that direction. Who could it be? She wasn't expecting anyone. "I think there's someone at my door," she said to Nancy. "Let me call you back later."

"Okay." The line went dead.

Emily rose from the couch and padded to the door. She looked through the peephole to see who it was.

Her heart sank.

What was the landlord doing here? He'd only come around the first time she'd moved in, and their communication since then was a brief acknowledgement from him whenever she wired the rent. Emily had been lucky to secure a monthly lease for the place at an affordable price, given how close it was to downtown Dexington. She had never missed any rent payments since she moved in. What could the problem be?

She removed the chain latch and swung the

door open. "Good afternoon, Mr. Baines," Emily said.

Mr. Baines gave her a toothy grin. "Afternoon, miss."

Emily moved aside to let him in. Mr. Baines was in his seventies and couldn't possibly harm her. "Is everything okay? I know my rent is due in a few days."

Mr. Baines dismissed her invitation. "No need for me to come in, miss. That's what I came to talk to you about."

"What is it, Mr. Baines?"

Mr. Baines wrung his hands and then sighed. "I'll need you to move out, miss."

Emily's heart skipped a beat. Did she just hear him correctly? "Why? Is there any problem?"

"My nephew's wife has been admitted at Dexington Healthcare for cancer treatment, and her treatment journey is going to be a long one. I wish I had a better option, but this apartment is the only place my nephew can stay, and it's close to the hospital." Mr. Baines pulled out a handkerchief from his pocket and wiped away the sweat on his brow. "I know this is a big inconvenience for you, so I'll refund you two months' rent in addition to your security deposit."

Emily's shoulders slumped. The news couldn't have come at a worse time. She didn't have a job, and now she soon wasn't going to have a roof over her head. But she'd never had any problems with Mr. Baines, and he was the only one willing to rent her a place despite her lack of rental or credit history.

"When would you need the apartment?" she asked.

"Tomorrow."

"Tomorrow? That's too soon!" This was even worse than she'd thought.

"I'm sorry, miss. Everything happened so quickly. I'm more than happy to write a recommendation letter on your behalf for your next landlord if that helps."

"But where would I go?"

"The rent refund should cover the cost of a good hotel till you find a place you like. And I did tell you when I was renting out the place that I'd originally kept it for family, and there was a possibility I might need it again. It's spelled out in the rental agreement."

Emily had forgotten about the clause. She'd

been so keen to get the place that it hadn't mattered at the time.

"I'll wire the money to you this afternoon," Mr. Baines said. "I have to go now." He patted her arm. "You take care, miss." And then he was gone.

Emily shut the door and leaned against it. What was she going to do now? A day that had started with hope and promise seemed to only get worse by the moment. She'd planned to use this afternoon looking for a job, but now she had to spend the time packing up her things. Fortunately, there were not a whole lot of them— she'd only brought the bare necessities with her and had left everything behind in New Jersey.

Emily sighed as she straightened. This was not the time to dally. The room was not going to pack itself.

Emily took one more look at the apartment that had been her happy place and shut the door for the final time. She lifted the box that contained the last of her items and carried it all the way to the front of the building where her car was parked. With the money the landlord had wired, her savings would now be enough to make her last tuition payment and cover the first rent and security deposit for a new place, but there was little left for anything else.

Her plan was to live out of her car in the meantime. There was a small drive-in movie theatre a few blocks away that seemed secure. Emily would job-hunt during the day and sleep in her car there at night.

She hadn't heard back from the Christmas farm, though she'd kept her phone close all day and night, which probably meant she didn't get the job. But her job search this morning had not been in vain. Emily had seen an advert online for an opening at a local dress shop in down-town Dexington and called ahead to find out more about it. The owner had asked her to come in immediately for an interview, and she had to be there in the next fifteen minutes.

Emily stuffed the box in the trunk and slid into the driver's seat. She turned the ignition.

There was no response.

No, not now. This shouldn't be happening. She'd even had the car serviced last week. Emily tried again, but the engine refused to turn over.

She dropped her head against the steering wheel. Just when she thought things couldn't get any worse. First it was her job, then her apartment, and now her car.

Tears burned at the back of Emily's eyes. She couldn't do this alone. This was all too much for her. *Help me, God!*

The shrill tone of her phone pierced the air.

CHAPTER 12

Geoffrey motioned to the maid and soon the clatter of plates and cutlery filled the air as she cleared the dining table.

Helen and Alex Dexington got up from the table and moved over to the living area, where a tea set waited next to the large white sofa. Geoffrey followed them. Soon a chocolatey woody aroma filled the air as he poured cups of tea for Alex and Helen.

"This is very nice," Helen said, her platinum blonde hair very much in place as she sipped her tea. She was dressed in a pink cashmere sweater paired with cream pants, and her diamond ear studs twinkled as she took another sip. "There's a floral note to this tea's flavor."

"It's the Vintage Narcissus tea, ma'am," Geoffrey said. "The tea expert sent it yesterday." Helen had become a tea connoisseur after she was advised by the doctor to minimize her coffee intake, and this was one of the few teas she hadn't yet tasted. Geoffrey spent some of his work time tracking down teas she hadn't tried. But she had yet to make him a tea drinker, though Alex had been quick to convert. But that was the way things were between Alex and Helen—they showed interest in whatever the other person loved.

"Let's get more of it, shall we?" Alex said to Geoffrey.

"Yes, sir."

Soon Alex finished his tea, dropped his cup on its saucer, and stood up. "I'll be right back, dear," he said to Helen as he leaned forward and gave her a kiss on the cheek. Then he turned to Geoffrey. "Let's go to my office," he said.

Alex's tall distinguished frame in a turtleneck and slacks was a sight to behold as he led Geoffrey through the large French doors on the north side of the living room, down the chandelier-lit hallway, and to Alex's office at the back of the house. Soon they were seated across from each other, a large vintage oak desk between them.

Geoffrey waited to hear what Alex had to say. They had already reviewed the estate accounts yesterday, so that couldn't be it.

"What's going on, Geoffrey?" Alex asked, his kind blue eyes searching Geoffrey's face.

"What do you mean, sir?"

"You've been absentminded since you got back yesterday. Is there something on your mind?"

Geoffrey shook his head. "Nothing at all, sir." There was no way he was going to tell Alex he hadn't heard back from Steve and didn't know whether or not he'd offered Emily Roth the job. If he so much as breathed the word, Alex would assume there was something between Emily and him, and then Helen would hear about it, and his life as he knew it would be officially over. Geoffrey would be engaged, married, and having a baby before anyone could say Jack Robinson.

He'd never seen anyone jump on the marriage bandwagon as fast as Helen, which was made worse by the fact that Phillip, Alex's and Helen's son, didn't seem particularly interested in settling down anytime soon.

So Geoffrey kept his mouth shut. He didn't need the misunderstanding, and besides, there was nothing between him and Miss Roth, even though her touch had sent his skin buzzing.

"You know you can talk to me," Alex said.

"It's really nothing, sir."

"If you say so." Alex studied Geoffrey for a moment, and Geoffrey fought the urge to squirm. "Work isn't the only important thing in life," Alex finally said. "You need a good woman too."

"I'll work on it, sir."

"See that you do. You know you can always come to me at any time. My door is always open," Alex finished.

"Thank you, sir."

Alex pulled an envelope from his desk drawer and handed it to Geoffrey. "Here's your stock portfolio statement. Eric sent it along with ours." Erik was the investment manager that handled the vast Dexington financial portfolio. Geoffrey had agreed to have him take care of his as well.

"Thank you, sir, and thanks again for the shares."

"Oh, it's nothing. Your father saved my life many years ago, and I promised him on his deathbed that I would take care of you as my own."

Geoffrey's father had been the family's butler before him. Alex had put some shares from the Dexington estate in Geoffrey's name, and the portfolio had grown till it was now worth billions of dollars. "And remember you don't have to keep working here unless you want to," Alex continued. "I'm more than happy to have you stay since you're like a son to me, but you'll always be a part of this family no matter what you decide."

"I'm fine, sir." Geoffrey really was. This family was the only one he had left, and Alex and Helen truly treated him like their own. Geoffrey also loved his job as his father had before him, so there really was no reason to leave.

"Great. Let's go back before Helen hunts us down. I can imagine you don't want her knowing anything about what we discussed."

Geoffrey grinned. "Yes, sir."

"That's what I thought."

"I know we're not doing much this year for Christmas, since Alex and I have one more trip to Europe before the year ends," Helen said. Alex and Geoffrey had returned to the living room, and Alex was now seated next to her. Geoffrey had taken the opposite chair. "I imagine Phillip is busy as well."

"He's very focused on the new product launch, ma'am," Geoffrey said. "He hasn't mentioned if he would be going to the orphanage this year as usual."

"I'm sure he will," Alex said. "He loves those kids."

"As he should. But he needs a family of his own," Helen replied.

"I totally agree. This house needs grandchildren running through it."

Helen gave Geoffrey a pointed look. "And that includes you. Geoffrey, when are we going to meet your special lady?"

Geoffrey shrugged. "Soon?"

Helen wagged a finger at him. "That's the

answer you've been giving me all these years, but it's going to end this time. If you don't bring her to me by the New Year, I'll find one for you!"

Geoffrey shot a glance at Alex.

Alex grinned. "I can't help you there," he said. "You're long overdue. When I was your age, Phillip was already in his teens. It's time to get the show on the road."

This was bad. If Helen had her eyes on a project, she saw it through. Geoffrey had no desire to become one.

"I mean it," Helen said to Geoffrey. "I'll put an ad in the newspaper for a bride for you if I don't meet her by the end of the year."

Yikes. This was worse than he thought. He had to derail Helen's train of thought fast. "So about the Christmas plans—"

"How about this?" Helen interrupted. "I'm supposed to be part of the Christmas festival planning committee this year, but Alex and I won't be around." Helen leaned forward. "Why don't you stand-in for me on the committee?" she said in an eager tone.

He could do that. It was just like every other committee, right? But why did he sense that Helen had something else up her sleeve?

"You have to be fully involved," Helen insisted. "You know I wouldn't expect anything less."

"Of course," Geoffrey responded.

"Why the committee? I thought we were discussing finding Geoffrey a wife," Alex said to Helen.

Geoffrey let out a sigh. Just when he thought he had dodged the bullet, Alex had him in his sights again.

"Oh, I haven't forgotten," Helen said as she gave Alex a conspiratorial wink. "I heard from Janet Jolley that a lot of eligible young ladies signed up for the committee this year." Janet Jolley was an active member of the Dexington local council and served as head of multiple committees.

Blast it. So that was what this was all about.

"Janet's daughter, who'd been unattached for quite some time, joined the committee last year and met her husband there," Helen continued. "So all the single ladies are hoping the same would happen for them."

Great. So he was going to be like a bull on display.

Helen gave Geoffrey a determined look. "So it's settled, right?"

"Yes, ma'am." He supposed he could play his role on the committee as long as there were no pulling or prodding.

Even if it happened, Geoffrey had gone through worse in his life.

He could survive this.

CHAPTER 13

"*M*ay I speak with Emily Roth?" the authoritative voice on the other end of the line asked.

"This is Emily Roth." Could it be …?

"This is Hilda Wilcox, the HR manager at the Holly Hoo Christmas Farm."

Emily's heart pounded. *Please, God, let it be good news.*

"Congratulations! You've been hired as a marketing assistant for the Holly Hoo Christmas Farm. Will you be accepting the offer?"

Emily swallowed. *My goodness.* She hadn't heard wrong—she'd gotten the job, despite the weird interview and Mr. Hart. Of course she was taking it! "Yes, I will," she said in a controlled voice that belied her happiness.

"Great. Welcome to the Holly Hoo family. We're excited to have you join us. Please expect the employment offer and on-boarding package in your email in the next five minutes. Would it be possible for you to come by today and get started on the paperwork?"

"Yes, I'll be there," Emily confirmed.

"Fantastic. Once again, congratulations, and see you soon."

"Thank you." The line disconnected.

Emily laid her head back on the headrest and allowed the news to sink in. She really had a job now!

Tears welled up behind her eyes. Just when she'd thought there was no hope, a light had shone in the tunnel. "Thank you, God," she whispered.

She stayed that way for a few minutes. Emily could feel all the weariness and tiredness seeping out of her body. Then she straightened, reinvigorated. Time to head to the farm.

Emily turned the ignition, but the car still wouldn't start.

She chuckled. Somehow the car issue didn't

matter as much anymore. What a difference good news could make!

Emily stepped out of the car.

There was no way she was going to lose this opportunity. Hound dogs were not strong enough to stop her from hightailing it to the farm and making sure the job stayed hers.

Hilda Wilcox looked up as Emily entered her office. "Come in, sit," she said and gestured to the visitors' chair across from her. "Would you like anything? Water? Coffee?"

"No, thank you," Emily said as she settled into the chair. So Hilda was the same lady who had escorted her yesterday from the lobby to the interview room.

Hilda beamed at her. "Congratulations and welcome to Holly Hoo Christmas Farm!"

"Thank you," Emily responded with a smile.

"We're so glad you could join us. This is a wonderful company to work for, and I'm sure you'll enjoy your time with us. Do you have any questions for me at this time?"

"None that I can think of."

"Sounds good. Why don't I walk you through all the paperwork?"

"Sure, that would be great."

For the next forty-five minutes, Hilda explained what each form was for and gave Emily time to fill each one.

Then Hilda placed a final set of papers before her.

Emily's eyes widened. "What's this?"

"It's exactly what it says. A rental agreement."

Emily's heart thudded. "Why would I need to sign a rental agreement?"

"For an apartment, of course. This job comes with housing if you want it. You don't pay any actual rent, and gas, water, and electricity are already included. The rental agreement is to make sure you take care of the place."

Unbelievable. Someone must be playing pranks on her. An apartment for this junior-level job? There had to be a catch somewhere.

"How is that possible?"

"We've had staff of all levels who have made use of the apartment one time or the other, especially when they've moved newly into town and have no place to stay."

A knock sounded on the door, and it opened and Peter stepped in. "I have some mail for you that was just delivered," he said and dropped the mail on Hilda's desk.

"Thank you," Hilda responded. Turning back to Emily, "So do you want the apartment?"

"I'm not sure if I have the right to take it," Emily said.

"Is this the penthouse?" Peter asked.

Penthouse? That was more reason to reject the place.

"Yes," Hilda said. "Emily here doesn't believe she can use the apartment."

"Oh, you can," Peter said. "You wouldn't be the first employee to use the place. The company likes to take care of its people."

"See what I mean?" Hilda said. "Thanks, Peter."

"My pleasure. I have to head back to the lobby." With that, he left the office.

"So have you made a decision?" Hilda asked.

There was no need to look a gift horse in the mouth—she would accept it as a blessing. Now Emily didn't have to worry about where she would sleep.

"I'll take it," she said.

"Awesome. Here's where you need to sign ..."

~

Even though she wasn't supposed to officially start until Monday, Emily stayed at her cubicle to read through the existing company documents that had already been pulled together for her. By the time she looked up, most of the employees had left for the day.

She closed the binder she'd been reading and locked up all the documents. She'd resisted checking out the apartment earlier, but now seemed a good time as any.

Emily picked up her coat and handbag, headed to the elevators, rode it to the topmost floor, and got off. There was only one set of doors, which meant the penthouse covered the whole floor. Talk about an upgrade.

She opened the apartment and stepped in. Emily stood in the middle of what was the center of the living area and stared around in disbelief.

The place was large, spacious, and pleasantly

designed with light blue and brown furnishings. The fresh scent of pine filled the air. She explored the rest of the space and discovered it had an office, a laundry room, a large kitchen, a master suite, and two other smaller bedrooms. All that was left was for her to bring her things over.

That was the real issue, right? Finding a way to get from the farm to her car, fix it, and then use it to move her belongings.

Her other options were limited. Most car rental places were closed by now except for the airport, and that was too far away. She hadn't had time to study the bus routes into the city, and Peter had confirmed that taxis were hard to find in the area. Maybe she could catch a ride into the city with one of the employees she'd met if she hurried.

Emily locked the apartment and raced toward the elevators. But when she arrived at the front of the building, the parking lot was almost empty.

Her shoulders slumped. She had only one option now: head to the bus stop a few miles away and hope the next bus arrived soon.

Emily looked down at her feet. She'd forgotten to include a pair of flats in her handbag, and with these high heels, she was in for a long walk. Hopefully, they wouldn't fall apart by the time she arrived at the bus stop.

She wrapped her coat tightly around her and began walking toward the farm's main gate. The air was slightly chilly, and Emily burrowed her hands deeper into the pockets of her coat.

She inhaled a deep cleansing breath as she took one step after another. It wasn't all bad. The walk would give her enough time to think, something she hadn't done in recent times.

The memory of the interview came to mind. It still surprised her that she had gotten the offer. She'd tried hard to find out why she'd been selected, but the HR manager had given her a quizzical look, so Emily had dropped it.

But she still found it puzzling. Maybe she'd been the owner's choice, though his weird chainsaw question had thrown her for a loop. Yes, that had to be it, because there was no way Mr. Hart would have wanted her to get the job.

The sound of an approaching car from behind her reached her ears, but Emily kept walking. It was probably someone she didn't know.

The car pulled up ahead of her and honked.

Emily stopped and watched as the window of a black SUV slid down.

"Hello, Miss Roth," a familiar voice said.

Emily tensed. Him again? Could these chance meetings just stop? She resumed walking, her face focused on the main gate up ahead.

But the car rolled along with her. "Would you like a ride into the city?" Mr. Hart asked. "The bus stop is quite far away."

Was he kidding? She would rather deal with bunions than enter his car. "No, thank you," she responded.

"Okay, suit yourself." He raised his window and sped off.

Emily stared at the car in consternation. Why had he even bothered to offer her a ride if he wasn't keen on giving her one? He was probably still upset that she'd gotten the job.

Yet, why did a little part of her wish she could learn more about him, even though it was obviously a terrible idea?

Get a grip, Emily. She didn't need a man in her life. She'd barely managed to escape and survive from the hands of one. She should know better by now.

Emily watched as the car disappeared beyond the main gates. She would find her own way back to the city no matter how long it took.

And hopefully, she'd never see Mr. Hart again.

CHAPTER 14

The corners of Geoffrey's mouth turned up slightly as he drove away from her. He was pretty sure she hadn't expected him to just leave and could still see her watching him from the rearview mirror. His response had probably irked her, but he hadn't been able to help himself.

But she'd made her choice, and that wasn't his fault. Unfortunately, her feet and pretty calves were going to pay for it—yes, he had noticed how lovely her legs were with those high heels, and he wasn't even a leg kind of guy.

But why was he noticing things about her that he hadn't about any other woman? She was stunning—he had to give her that—but he met beautiful women all the time. What was it about her that drew his attention?

Geoffrey dwelt on it for a moment, yet no answers came. But should he really be thinking about her? They had no business together, and he'd only come to the farm to retrieve a poetry book he'd left behind in the apartment for the few times when he'd needed privacy away from the Dexington estate. The book had been a gift from his mom before her death, a memento he cherished. Sure, he'd been the one to recommend the apartment for Miss Roth's use when he remembered what her friend had said about her rent situation. But he'd done that anonymously to make up for what happened with her last job. Now, he didn't owe her anymore, so there was really no reason for them to cross paths again.

Even though she'd sprung to mind more times than he cared to admit in the past few days.

And something within him was curious about her.

Yet their association had to end here. He was content with his life and his work and didn't need a woman in it, especially one he knew nothing about.

Geoffrey glanced once more at the distant figure in his rearview mirror.

Then he drove away.

CHAPTER 15

Emily collapsed on her new bed. *Ah!* She was finally done for the day. Her car was fixed, and she'd moved in all her stuff. The place already felt like home, though most of the things in it came with the apartment. All she needed now was a long shower and a good night's sleep, but she found it hard to muster up enough strength to even move a finger. Maybe she should just rest for a bit …

Emily clawed at the man's hands around her throat, but they remained strong no matter how much she pulled at them. This time he meant to kill her.

Her vision spun, and her breath grew ragged. Marrying Calvin, had been the worst mistake of her life, a decision she would forever regret. She'd endured the years of abuse, but this time it was different. She had another life to protect. With a strength she didn't think possible, Emily kicked his groin.

The man groaned as his hands loosened momentarily around her neck. But then he pushed her in a fit of rage.

Emily reached out, hands trying to grab anything to break her fall. She caught the front of his shirt, pulling him along.

She cried out in pain as her body first hit the steps, and soon they tumbled down the stairs, his heavy weight pressed against her, till they landed at its foot. Calvin lay motionless beside her. A searing pain tore through Emily's stomach, and she doubled over. *Please God, no …*

Emily's eyes jerked open, and she sat up, chest heaving and heart pounding. Her blouse was drenched in sweat despite the cool air from the central air conditioning system.

She took quick deep breaths till she felt her heart rate returning to normal. It had been a while since she'd had this nightmare. So why now? Was it an ominous sign? No, that wasn't possible. That chapter of her life was over.

She looked around the unfamiliar environment, and then she remembered where she was. Her new apartment. A good place for her to start over again. She still had her eye out for the Dexington Healthcare job once she was qualified, but her first impressions of the farm were good. The HR manager had even hinted that she could become full-time with a better pay grade in less than six months, especially if she performed well on the job during the Christmas season.

Emily forced herself off the bed and wandered over to the large window. She swept the curtains open and stared outside. Dawn was breaking, and the world looked beautiful, untainted like a newborn, and filled with promise.

Thank goodness she could live here as long as she wanted. The key was to make herself indispensable.

Emily resolved to start off by spending most of the day coming up with detailed creative ideas that the farm could quickly implement.

Then she would take a break to attend the Christmas festival planning meeting.

CHAPTER 16

The chairs were already filled with volunteers when Geoffrey entered the community hall that early evening. He'd arrived on time, which meant lots of people were excited about the Christmas festival. It wasn't surprising given that he'd heard last year's was a resounding success. The town loved its community events, and the Christmas ones were no exception.

Geoffrey searched the rows of seats till he found an empty one in the front. He'd just sat down when the stage's side door opened, and the town's community event leader, a tall graceful lady in sweater and jeans tucked into knee-high winter boots, entered and took the stage. She rapped her knuckle on the podium, and the room quietened.

"Thank you everyone for coming," she said, in a voice used to commanding an audience. "For those who don't know me, I'm Janet Jolley, and I'm the chairperson in charge of the Christmas festival this year." A smattering of applause followed. "Before we get started, I'd like Ms. Parker to lead us in prayer. Ms. Parker?"

The sixty-something-year-old widow was a staunch member of the community and had served as a long-time organist for one of the churches in the area. Her lilting voice led the opening prayer as all heads bowed and all eyes closed. Then the prayer was over, and then all eyes were back on Ms. Jolley.

"Thank you once again for coming," Ms. Jolley said. "We're so excited you could join us this year to help plan the Christmas festival event. Instead of letting everyone introduce themselves, we have an attendance sheet circulating through the group right now. Please add your name and your phone number to the list. Some of you were here last year, and we hope to leverage the same process again. We'll be splitting the group into ..."

Ms. Jolley was remarkably efficient with her words, considering that politicians weren't particularly known for their succinct speeches. Geoffrey watched with interest as she provided an overview of the Christmas festival.

The festival would take place next week in an adjacent community center that had been under repair for the past year but was now ready for use. A smaller committee had already been at work for a few weeks behind the scenes, and most of the vendors had already been contracted. There would be a face painting station, a Christmas story reading grove for little kids, a hot cocoa stand, an inflatable snow globe photo booth, a candy cane runway, a corner for wreath making, and many other booths and activities. The whole event sounded exciting, and Geoffrey could see Ms. Jolley pulling it off successfully.

After her speech, the volunteers were divided into teams with meeting points at designated areas of the hall. Geoffrey ended up on the decorating team, which was responsible for sprucing up the center. They were told a cleaning crew had already been through to make sure the place was ready.

Geoffrey moved over to where his team had gathered and greeted the other members already there. Most of them were familiar to him since he'd met them at one time or the other. Then he noticed they all had one characteristic in common. They were either single or widowed!

He shook his head in amazement and chuckled. How had they managed it? There hadn't been enough time to curate that from the attendance list, which probably meant some folks had taken it upon themselves to identify them before the meeting started. It was as Helen had said—there was this whole other matchmaking play going on in the background, and he was pretty certain Ms. Jolley was right in the thick of things. If only it were that easy to find that special one. Well, he hoped it worked out for them as long as they left him out of it.

Geoffrey noticed the other teams had started their meetings. Where was his team's leader? Ms. Jolley had told them the leader would identify himself as soon as the team gathered, but his team members seemed to be looking at each other.

"Welcome to the Decorating team," a quiet but confident voice said from behind him.

Geoffrey turned.

His heart skipped a beat.

The last person he'd expected to see was standing in front of him, looking adorable in blue skinny jeans and a cream turtleneck, her blonde hair held up in a ponytail.

Despite himself, Geoffrey chuckled. Something was definitely going on.

Because if not, what was she doing here?

CHAPTER 17

*E*mily's eyes met Geoffrey's and widened. Him again? Of all the luck in the world, he had to show up in her team.

She hadn't wanted the leadership spot. She avoided being in the limelight, because it reminded her too much of how Calvin used to show her off in front of his friends. But Nancy had said planning the Christmas festival had been so much fun last year, and was sad she couldn't participate this year due to Perry's condition. So she'd recommended Emily instead to take her place, and Emily had agreed despite her hesitation. The rest was history.

Emily had been surprised how easily other members of the committee had accepted her and made her feel welcome. It reminded her how much she'd loved planning and organizing activities in high school before she met Calvin. As much as Emily shied away from anything Christmasy, the committee turned out to be a good opportunity to put herself out there and meet people, something she was working on. She'd enjoyed it and ended up staying, so here she was.

But she hadn't bargained for Geoffrey, and now her pulse raced at his nearness. This wasn't good. She had a job to do, and she couldn't allow those beautiful brown eyes to distract her.

She noticed a young man standing next to Geoffrey gawking at her like a lovesick puppy. It was interesting she still had an effect on anyone, considering that Calvin had made it his mission to get it into her head that she was worthless without him. Unfortunately, he'd somewhat succeeded. Emily had ended up spending the last few months rebuilding her confidence and self-worth.

She gave the young man a warm smile, and his ears turned red.

"Hello, I'm Teddy," he managed to say.

"Nice to meet you, Teddy." Then she turned to the rest of the group.

"Thank you for agreeing to be part of the Decorating team. I'm Emily Roth, and I'm your team leader. Ms. Jolley gave a brief overview earlier of what we would expect the event to look like. Our job is to make it better than that. And as she said, there's no cleaning involved as far as I'm aware—I know some of us hate cleaning of any sort." The group chuckled. "Why don't we head to the event center and get right down to it? Please follow me."

Emily took them through the stage's side door, down a narrow hallway, and through another door that opened into the event center. Even though she'd seen the space before, Emily was still amazed at how open and extensive the area was, large enough to accommodate the crowd they expected next week.

She led the team to a corner where bags and bags of decorations were stacked, and turned to address them. "We are going to divide ourselves into three groups for today's work. One group will be responsible for hanging up the garlands, red bows, and golden bells. If you look up, you'll see stick-on hooks placed at intervals on the wall. That's where each bow and matching bell will be hung. Keep in mind that the restrooms are also going to get the same treatment.

"The second group will be responsible for putting up all the Christmas lights both inside and outside the hall, while the final group will be responsible for decorating the Christmas tree, which should arrive any moment from now."

"Miss Roth, can I speak to you for a moment?"

Emily turned to see Janet Jolley standing a few feet away from her. "Please go ahead and decide what group you'd like to join," she said to her team. "I'll be right back."

She headed to where Janet waited. "Is everything okay?" she asked.

"There's a problem I need to discuss with you," Janet said.

Emily listened as Janet outlined the issue. It wasn't exactly what her team had signed up for, but it could be done, and it was better to address the issue immediately. "Okay, we'll take care of it."

She saw the look of relief cross Janet's face.

"Thank you," Janet said. "Let me know if you have any issues."

"Sure, will do."

Janet smiled at her, turned, and headed toward the exit.

Emily made her way back to the team. This was a tricky assignment. Who could she get to handle this? She would have taken care of it herself, but two decorating vendors were supposed to stop by shortly. She had to find someone who could handle it quickly to prevent any delays.

Her eyes scanned the team and then stopped. A small smile tugged at the corners of her lips.

Emily had just found the perfect person.

Geoffrey noticed Emily zero in on him. He still hadn't gotten over the fact she was right here in front of him. Now, something about the glint in her eye told him she was up to something.

"Okay, have we decided which group we want to work in?" Emily asked the team.

His shoulders relaxed. Maybe he'd guessed wrong about her intentions.

"Yes, we have," Teddy responded. Everyone else nodded their assent.

"Great," Emily said. "The blue bags are for team one, the red bags for team two, and the yellow bags for team three. We have about two hours to work on this, so let's plan to regroup in an hour-forty-five minutes' time. Thank you, everyone."

Geoffrey had chosen group two—he'd hung the Christmas lights multiple times over the years at the Dexington estate, and the experience would come in handy. He bent to lift one of the red bags.

"Mr. Hart, could I talk to you for a second?" Emily asked. Geoffrey straightened and looked at her. "In private, please."

What could this be about? Okay, maybe she wanted him to pretend they didn't know each other before, which was totally fine by him. That way he didn't have to explain how they first met, which was an incident he had no desire to share.

Geoffrey followed her to another area of the room. "What is it, Miss Roth?"

"I hope you don't mind that I've taken you away from your group, but I do have a task that the team has just been asked to take care of."

Now why was she avoiding his eyes? He had a bad vibe about this.

"I figured you were the best man for the job,

and the only one I could ask this favor," she continued.

Him? Really? This had to be an unpleasant task. He couldn't imagine Ms. Roth thinking kindly about him.

"What is it?" he asked.

"Could you clean up the men's toilet in preparation for the decorations? It's such a mess right now."

Bingo! He'd been right. She made it sound as if it was no big deal, but it was the toilet for goodness sake, and a task that no one else in the group would want to touch with a ten-foot pole. This was no doubt a revenge for their previous run-ins.

But he could do this. Challenge accepted. "Where are the supplies?" he asked.

Her eyes widened. He supposed his response wasn't what she had expected. "They should be in the bathroom."

"Right. I'll take care of it immediately." He didn't wait for her response and headed back to the corner, where Teddy had just grabbed the last red bag. "Teddy, I've been reassigned to take care of something else. I'll catch up with you guys as soon as I'm done."

Teddy nodded and left with the bag.

Geoffrey rolled up his sleeves. Luckily, he'd washed a toilet or two before, so he knew his way around them.

It was time to show Ms. Roth what he was truly made of.

$\mathcal{E}$mily watched Geoffrey head off to the restrooms. She didn't know what she'd been expecting from him, but it wasn't this.

His response instead made her feel bad about what she had done. Had it been mean and childish of her? She wasn't typically like this, but something about Geoffrey just brought out this response from her.

She brushed the guilt away from her mind. Oh well, someone had to do it, and it might end up being a good experience for him to take care of something that regular folks were used to doing.

Emily heard the sound of the main doors open, and she turned in that direction. Two men were rolling in a very large Christmas tree. She'd never seen one this size in person before. As they neared her, she did a double take.

"Hi, Emily," Steve said with a grin on his face as they rolled the tree to a stop before her.

Emily gave him a warm smile. "Hello, Mr. Henshaw. I didn't expect to see you here."

"We grow Christmas trees, remember? And it's Steve, and this is Mark. Mark, Emily is one of our new employees."

"Hello, Mark, nice to meet you." Emily said.

"Same here," said the grizzly man with a full beard. Maybe it was a trend of some sort to grow facial hair at the farm. It wouldn't surprise her, given Santa also had a full one.

Emily smiled. "Glad to see you both here. I don't know why I didn't make the connection when I was told to expect a Christmas tree."

Steve looked around. "Nice hall. So where should we put this?"

"Oh, this way." Emily led them to the area marked for the tree's placement. Steve and Mark moved the Christmas tree to its designated spot, and then Mark went back out through the doors.

"He's gone to bring some ladders for you guys," Steve said. "The committee requested we loan two of them to you so you could use it to decorate the tree. You'll have to sign for them."

"No problem." She'd make sure they were stored away once her team was done with them. "Thank you again for the job."

"It wasn't me."

Emily gave him a quizzical look. "What do you mean?"

"You did great at the interview, and you were one of our finalists. But Geoffrey made an impassioned request for us to select you."

Mr. Hart did? Why? "I thought he didn't—"

"Whatever happened between you two?" Steve leaned forward, his blue eyes twinkling with mischief.

Emily hid a smile. "It's not my story to tell."

Steve sighed. "You two are hiding something, and I'm going to find out eventually. I've never seen him this way before. What have you done to my friend?"

What was Steve talking about? He probably had it all wrong.

Steve glanced around the hall. "By the way, where is the man in question? He told me he'd be here."

"Ehm ... he is working in the restroom."

Steve burst out in laughter. "And I suppose you assigned him to it."

"Well, it turned out that way."

"This was some kind of payback, right? Now, I really want to know what happened between you two."

"It's nothing, really."

By now, Mark had returned with the ladders, a sheet of paper, and a pen. He handed the paper and pen to Emily. "Please sign here," he said.

Emily accepted both items, signed the sheet, and handed them back to him.

"Okay, I think we're done here," Steve said. "We still have some other trees to deliver around town. Good to see you, Emily."

"Same here. Have a good weekend."

"I will, and say hello to Geoffrey when he comes out," he said with a smile in his voice.

"Will do. See you on Monday."

Steve gave her a wave over his head as he walked away with Mark.

Emily watched them leave, and then motioned to team three to start work on the tree.

It had been nice to see Steve again. She'd had no idea that Geoffrey had advocated for her.

Now she truly felt terrible for making him clean the toilets.

How was she going to make it up to him?

Soon, the team finished their work for the day and assembled back at the center of the hall. The ladders and any remaining items from the bags had been dropped off in the storage room adjacent to the hall's emergency exit.

Emily looked around. The center had already taken on a festive vibe with the twinkling lights, red ribbons, and a beautiful Christmas tree shining with gold, silver, and red ornaments.

"This looks great," she said. "Good job, everyone. We'll stop here for today and meet again same time next week Friday to install the outstanding decorations that the vendors will bring in. Sound good?" There was a chorus of responses as everyone expressed their agreement. "Awesome. Thanks, everyone, and have a great weekend." With that, Emily closed the meeting.

The team dispersed immediately, though some folks hung back to meet and greet each other, while others strolled toward the exit. Emily spied Geoffrey heading her way.

Not now. She was too embarrassed to face him.

Emily turned away instead and strode in the direction of the Christmas tree.

A hand touched her arm, and Emily felt a buzz of electricity flow through her skin. She didn't need to look to know who it was.

She turned to face him. Geoffrey didn't appear any worse for the wear. Instead, one would think he'd been chilling out instead of scrubbing the toilet. Only a strong scent of pine gave him away.

"Would you care for a cup of coffee with me, Ms. Roth?"

The room almost fell silent at Geoffrey's voice, and Emily felt curious eyes staring at them.

Her mouth went dry. She hated being the center of attention. Calvin had loved to be noticed, and Emily had come to detest every minute of it. She had to steer the limelight away from her.

"Sure," she said quietly.

"Good," he responded in a matching tone. "Let's meet in the coffee shop across the street in forty-five minutes."

He must have seen the hesitation in her face because he said, "You owe me for the toilets." He didn't wait for her response and headed off.

He had her right there. Maybe the coffee chat would be a good time to apologize for that. But wait! Forty-five minutes? Emily didn't need that long to wrap up here.

Her eyes searched around for Geoffrey, but he had already made his way across the room and was almost at the exit. Emily didn't want to race after him—it would only draw attention to her and prompt the town's rumor mill to start working hard on her behalf, which was the last thing she needed.

Okay, she would give him forty-five minutes and not a minute longer.

But what did he want to talk to her about?

CHAPTER 20

Geoffrey glanced at his watch as he headed into Dexington House. He had about fifteen minutes left till he had to meet Emily. He'd managed to get home in record time and take a much-needed shower after his short stint with the toilets. This was one meeting he couldn't afford to be late for—something told him she would not wait for him beyond that, and he had to speak with her. But first he needed to drop off a package for Phillip Dexington.

Geoffrey entered the mansion, made his way to Phillip's office, and knocked on the door.

"Come in," a voice answered from within. Geoffrey turned the knob and entered. Phillip was examining some papers at his desk and looked up. "Hey, Geoffrey. What's going on?"

Geoffrey showed him the package in his hand. "Something came in for you earlier today, sir."

"Ah, the package I've been waiting for. Just drop it here on the desk. Thanks."

Geoffrey deposited the mail. "I'll see you later, sir," he said.

Phillip leaned back against his leather swivel chair. "When are you going to stop calling me 'sir'?" He peered at Geoffrey. "Wait, is that a pair of jeans you're wearing? Who is the lucky lady?"

"What do you mean?"

Phillip chuckled. "Don't play dumb with me. You know exactly what I'm talking about. You, wearing jeans you've never worn before all these years? You're definitely trying to impress someone."

What was Phillip talking about? He wore jeans for time to time, just not in the main house. "Enjoy your day, sir," Geoffrey said and headed to the door.

Phillip laughed. "You know I'm right. Just

make sure Mother doesn't see you on your way out."

It would truly be a disaster if that happened. Helen would not let him rest till she ferreted out what was going on with him, which was a terrible idea since he didn't even know what that was yet. He'd had time to think while scrubbing the toilets and had decided that his constant run-ins with Miss Roth might not be a mistake. Something about her had gotten under his skin, and he was curious to explore it more.

Geoffrey closed the door to the office behind him and hurried out of the house.

Time was ticking, and he couldn't keep a lady waiting.

CHAPTER 21

Emily twiddled her fingers as she waited for Geoffrey to arrive. The hippy coffee shop was almost empty, which suited her just fine. But the smell of roast beef hung low in the air and caused her stomach to rumble. She had missed lunch without knowing it. The orange juice she was sipping would have to hold her till she got home.

She leaned back against her chair. What did Mr. Hart want with her? His request had popped out of the blue, and she'd been too shocked to say no. Though a certain part of her would argue that the idea of spending time with him wasn't disagreeable.

Emily glanced at her phone. His forty-five

minutes was almost up. She would give him five extra minutes, but then she was gone.

The doorbell jingled. Emily looked up to see Mr. Hart enter, and her pulse quickened. How could he look this good in a coat over button-down shirt and a pair of jeans? She noticed the few customers in the shop assessing him appreciatively. She looked down at herself—she looked frumpy in comparison.

Soon he reached her table, removed his coat, and sat down. "I hope I'm not late," he said. "Thanks for waiting."

Emily shook her head. "No, you're right on time."

"Good." He lifted his hand, and a waitress came over.

"How may I help you, sir?" the young lady asked.

"Could I have a cup of espresso with a cinnamon stick on the side?" he said. He glanced at Emily. "Would you like anything?" he asked.

She shook her head, still shocked at what she'd just heard. Unbelievable. How in the world was the guy sitting opposite her the only other person she'd met who loved the espresso-cinnamon combination?

"That will be all," he said to the waitress.

"Coming right up."

"Thanks." The waitress left.

Geoffrey must have noticed her staring. "What?" he asked. "Do I have something on my face?" He touched his jaw.

A thrill ran through Emily at the sight. Why did he have to draw attention to his jawline that was just pure perfection? "No … no no. It just … I've never met anyone else who liked cinnamon sticks with their espresso." There was no way she was telling him how everything about his face from his eyes to his lips and to his jawline were affecting her.

"It was a favorite of my parents, and then became mine too," he said.

"Funny, it was my mum's favorite too," Emily responded.

Geoffrey's fingers played with the edge of the napkin in front of him. "Is she back in New Jersey?"

"No, she died last year."

His hand stilled. "I'm sorry."

"It's okay."

The air became awkward, uncomfortable even. Fortunately, the waitress returned at that moment with his coffee. Geoffrey picked up the cinnamon stick and stirred the coffee with it before taking a sip.

"I'm surprised they have cinnamon sticks available," Emily said.

"I asked them to stock them."

Right. She'd forgotten he was supposed to be someone important—he was a patron at the boutique, which should have been her first clue.

Her stomach rumbled. Emily hoped Geoffrey hadn't heard it. But it served as a reminder that it was time to get the show on the road. "So why did you want to meet me?" she asked.

He took another sip of his coffee before answering. "I figured it might be a good idea to properly introduce ourselves to each other, since we got off on the wrong foot in previous inter-actions."

Now, Emily felt worse. She had to straighten things out. "I'm sorry I made you clean the toilets," she blurted out, and her cheeks heated up.

Geoffrey laughed, a deep musical note that wreaked delicious havoc on her emotions. What was wrong with her? "I figured it was payback," he responded. "No offense taken."

Her shoulders relaxed. She'd expected him to be angry or annoyed, but he found it funny instead. What a strange man. Now she was curious about him.

"I do want to apologize for making you lose your last job," Geoffrey said. "It was never my intention to mess with anyone's livelihood."

Emily smiled. "It was my fault anyway. I knew the rules, and I broke them. But that's in the past now."

"So truce?" he asked, extending his hand across the table for a handshake.

"Truce," she responded, accepting it.

A charge of electricity zapped through her at his touch and spread all the way to her toes. He held onto her hand for a bit longer than necessary, but interestingly enough, she didn't mind. Now what was wrong with her?

"I'm Geoffrey," he said. "Nice to meet you."

"I'm Emily. A pleasure to meet you too."

He let go of her hand then, and Emily felt a sudden loss at his touch. This was getting weirder and weirder. Why was she being affected like this by him?

"So what do you do, Geoffrey?"

"I'm a butler."

Emily's eyes widened. Who would have thought? Was that why he was at the boutique? But it would be rude to ask. "I had no idea butlers still existed in this century, no offense."

"We are definitely a dying breed. Does the job sound weird to you?"

"No. I think it's interesting, and you must be a patient man. But more importantly, do you love it?"

"I do, and I work with a really good family who treat me well."

"Does it pay you enough to take care of your needs?"

"Yes, it does."

"Then that's all that matters." Because that was what she was working toward: creating a life for herself that she was happy with.

"How about you?" Geoffrey said.

"You know about the Christmas farm job."

"If you had the choice of any career, what would you want? Don't worry, I won't say anything to Steve."

Could she trust him? Well, he'd helped her with the job, so he couldn't say otherwise now.

"My dream job is to work with Dexington Healthcare. They don't care about how old you are when you get a college degree."

"Yes, I remember you mentioned during the interview that you were getting your degree soon."

"Yes. I'm not ashamed that I'm only getting it now."

"You shouldn't be. It takes bravery to do, and I applaud that."

His words caused a warm feeling to curl up around her heart. She was really enjoying chatting with him. But she had to ask even though she wasn't interested in a relationship. "How old are you?" She could feel her ears heat up. "I mean, are you single? Sorry … I'm not trying to probe or anything, but I just …"

Geoffrey laughed. "I'm single."

"Really? I would have thought …?"

"I look too old?"

"You look hot!" Emily covered her mouth. "Sorry, I didn't mean to blurt that out."

Geoffrey leaned forward, the corners of his lips curling into a smile. "Are you applying?"

Emily felt her whole face heat up. "Just forget I said anything," she muttered. *I really stuck my foot in my mouth with that one,* she thought.

"I wouldn't mind," he said in a teasing tone.

Emily wished the ground could just open up and swallow her. She was sure her face was as red as a tomato now. He was clearly teasing her, though she appreciated the thought. It was time to flee before she embarrassed herself any further.

She glanced at her watch. It was getting late, and she still had work to do on the marketing ideas. "I have to go," she said.

"Can we do this again sometime?"

Emily stared at him in surprise. Was he serious? He was someone who could obviously have his choice of any lady. So why her? He clearly didn't know much about her, and she wasn't really keen on any romantic entanglements. But they could just be friends, right? A part of her didn't mind seeing him again. "Sure."

"Can I have your number?"

She nodded. "Your phone please."

He handed it to her, and she typed in her number and gave it back to him. "Here you go."

Then her phone began to buzz. She picked it up and looked at the screen.

"That's my number," he said.

"Great." Emily stood up and donned her coat. Geoffrey did the same as well.

"Can I drop you off?" he asked.

"There's no need. I have my car out front."

"Okay, I'll walk you to it."

Emily picked up her handbag and led the way out. She could sense eyes on them as they headed to the exit. *I'm sure they're wondering what this good-looking guy is doing with this dowdy lady,* she thought. But she didn't care. She was comfortable in these clothes, which was important to her after being forced to wear skin-tight attire for many years.

The sky had grown somewhat dark, but the streetlights were on, so Emily could still see her way. The December air was slightly nippy as expected, though there had been no snowfall so far.

Soon they arrived at her car. "I'll just get going," she said.

Geoffrey ran his hand through his hair. "This is your car?"

"Why do you ask?"

"It looks like a car that parked in my spot at the mall a few days ago."

She pointed a finger at him. "So you were the meanie that got my car towed?"

He held up his hands in mock surrender. "It was towed? Sorry, but you parked in my spot." A lazy smile lingered on his lips. "You seem to be quite the rule breaker, Miss Roth."

She'd never considered herself to be one. Her ex had had a million and one rules for her to follow, and it had been exhausting keeping track of each one, though she'd managed. If she was now breaking rules, didn't that mean she was coming out of her shell?

"It's Emily, thank you."

"Emily, I look forward to learning more about you."

If only he knew. She opened her door. "Enjoy your weekend, Geoffrey."

"I'll talk to you soon."

Emily nodded, got into her car, and drove away.

Emily yawned as she stretched out on the bed. It was comfy, and she didn't want to get up. Then she remembered her morning appointment and jumped up. She couldn't afford to be late.

She padded to the kitchen and turned on the coffee maker. Soon delicious coffee streamed down into her mug, and her first taste of it didn't disappoint.

Emily moved over to the windows and gazed out as she sipped her coffee. So this was what a peaceful morning of God's nature looked like—the sun rising in the blue picturesque sky and casting beautiful rays among the Christmas trees as they swayed slightly with the morning breeze. She could admire this view forever, but she had a place she needed to be.

She took a quick shower, dressed in a loose sweater and a pair of jeans, and headed out. Soon she arrived at St. Andrews orphanage, where she'd been volunteering since she arrived in Dexington. A little figure in a coat over her pajamas was waiting for her on the porch.

"Miss Emily!" the little four-year-old girl screamed and flew down the stairs.

Emily caught her in her arms and nuzzled her blonde hair. "How are you today, Hannah?"

The little girl grinned. "I've been waiting for you forever."

"She sure has." Emily looked up to see Elsie, the orphanage's cook, coming down the stairs. Emily hadn't even noticed her presence. "She has been on pins and needles since she woke up and has probably worn a hole through the porch floor."

"Thank you for waiting with her."

"My pleasure. You know this little one is special." She ruffled Hannah's hair, and the little girl giggled. "I'll be on my way now. I have a few items I need to grab from the grocery store."

"Thank you." Emily watched with Hannah

as Elsie entered her car and drove off. Then she turned to Hannah. "Now, let's get you all cleaned up, little one."

Thirty-minutes later, Emily was all dressed in a little purple frock, her hair done up in pigtails. She twirled in front of the mirror in the room. "I look pretty, Miss Emily," she said.

Emily smiled at Hannah's reflection. "Yes, you do."

"Can I go play now?"

Kids. She loved how their minds would quickly go from one thing to another. It was one of the reasons why she had always wanted one. A slice of pain cut through her heart at the thought, and she took a quick breath. The ache would never fully go away, but being here with the kids at the orphanage was a balm that made it easier for her to manage. Hannah had practically saved her. "Sure," Emily said.

Hannah skipped ahead out through the door and down the hallway, and Emily followed. She'd loved coming here to volunteer ever since she heard about the orphanage from the church she attended, and she made it her mission to show up every Saturday.

"Ouch!" a tiny voice cried out.

"Hannah!" Emily blamed herself for being distracted and letting the girl out of her sight. She rushed to where Hannah had landed on the floor. A man stooped next to her.

"Are you okay?" he asked Hannah.

Emily screeched to a halt.

She would have recognized that voice anywhere.

CHAPTER 23

Geoffrey looked up to see Emily standing a few feet away from him, her nearness and soft gardenia scent sending his heart racing.

"What are you doing here?" she asked.

That should have been his question. This was the last place he'd expected to see her. He had to admit she was a sight for sore eyes with those beautiful brown eyes, and her lovely hair rolled into a loose chignon. He'd thought about their coffee chat last night and had come to one conclusion: he was attracted to her—something that hadn't really happened with anyone else all these years. But he wasn't sure yet whether to pursue her or not. Being wealthy had made him a bit more cautious than usual.

"Uncle Goofy, I have a boo-boo."

He heard a chuckle. *Yes, go ahead and laugh all you want.* This was his nickname courtesy of Hannah, and he didn't mind it.

He turned his attention back to Hannah. "Let me see." She let him examine her knee. It was only a scratch. No bones were broken. "Okay, let's take care of it." He hoisted her into his arms and led the way to the living room. "Emily, could you get the first aid box?" He wasn't certain if she knew where it was kept at the orphanage, but she could always ask.

"Okay," she replied and headed off in the opposite direction.

Geoffrey entered the living room and set Hannah gently on the couch. "How are you feeling, Hannah?" he asked her.

"I'm fine. I like Miss Emily."

Only kids could string two very different sentences one after the other and expect it to make sense. "You do?"

"Yes. I don't know …. She is like a mommy. And I like her hugs too."

That was high praise coming from Hannah

and a positive check in Emily's favor. It seemed his instincts about her were not wrong.

"Is she always here?" he asked her.

"Hmmm …" Hannah cocked her head to the side. "Yes, she comes the day we don't have school or church."

Which meant every Saturday. "Was she here last Christmas?"

Hannah shook her head. "Uh-uh. She ate my birthday cake." Hannah's birthday was in February, so, Emily had been coming here a while. "Uncle Goofy?"

"Yes, Hannah?"

"I'm hungry."

"I thought you already had breakfast."

"But a cookie will make my boo-boo better."

Geoffrey chuckled. The little scamp. Hannah was famous for her sweet tooth.

"We'll see what Elsie says, okay?"

Hannah's face fell. "Okay."

Emily returned with the first aid box and handed it to Geoffrey. He was used to helping the boys with their cuts and scrapes, so he took care of Hannah's knee in no time.

"Thank you, Uncle Goofy," Hannah said, though her face remained crestfallen.

"You're welcome." Geoffrey turned to Emily. "Was the director in her office?" he asked.

"Martha? She's in the kitchen."

Perfect. She was the only other person who could authorize cookies for Hannah. "Hannah, Martha is in the kitchen," Geoffrey said. "You could ask her if you could get a cookie."

Her perfect face lit up. "Yay! Thank you, Uncle Goofy. You're the best." She gave him a hug and then ran toward the kitchen.

"You're spoiling her," Emily said with a smile.

He grinned. "That's what uncles are for." He got up from where he'd been kneeling and sat on the couch. "I didn't know you volunteered here."

Emily sat opposite him on a loveseat. "I started coming here earlier this year. How about you?"

"I've lost track of how long—must be over two decades."

"Wow, that's a long time."

Geoffrey shrugged. "It's been fun. But I mostly pop by during the week. Today was an exception since I had to drop something off on behalf of the family I work for."

"I love coming here. The kids are great."

"They really are, and they are so optimistic. Martha has done a great job raising them."

"I heard all those who grew up here come by to help."

"They do. It's one of the reasons this orphanage is so successful. They are like one big family. I feel like I'm the one getting blessed instead of them whenever I come here."

"Do you like kids?" Emily asked.

"Absolutely. I hope to have some of my own eventually."

"I love them. I wish ... never mind."

Geoffrey could hear the sorrow in her voice, and it seemed like there was some story behind it. Emily looked vulnerable, and he felt an urge to hug her and let her know it was going to be okay.

Stop it! he scolded himself. Emily was someone he barely knew. What was wrong with him?

Hannah raced back in that moment. "Miss Emily!"

Emily sucked in a breath and then turned to Hannah with a smile on her face. The moment was over, like it had never happened. "What is it, darling?"

"Can we go play with the princesses now?"

Geoffrey gave Emily a quizzical look. Princesses?

"Yes we can play with the dollhouse," Emily corrected, more for Geoffrey's benefit. Turning back to Geoffrey, "We have to go."

Hannah bounced on her feet. "Let's play princess, Uncle Goofy!"

This was one game he'd never played, but he was curious to see how it would work with Emily. "Okay."

Emily's eyes widened. "Are you sure?"

"Positive." Though he had no idea what he'd just signed up for. "Lead the way."

Geoffrey followed Emily and Hannah till they got to the children's playroom. A large princess dollhouse was all set up in one corner of the space, and Emily headed in that direction. Hannah ran ahead and pulled out a large pink box that was hidden behind the dollhouse. "Uncle Goofy, sit," she said.

Geoffrey followed Emily's direction and sat cross-legged on the floor in front of the dollhouse.

Hannah lifted a tiara from the box. "Uncle Goofy, you're a princess, and you need a tiara."

Geoffrey glanced at Emily who just chuckled. Okay, he could do this. How hard was it to be a princess?

He accepted the tiara and placed it on his head. He was pretty certain he looked ridiculous.

"Uncle Goofy, you have to sit like a princess!"

Geoffrey straightened his back and looked straight ahead. By now, Emily could barely hold back her laughter.

"Shush, Miss Emily," Hannah said in a stern tone.

"I'm sorry, Hannah. I won't laugh again," Emily said with seriousness, though the corners of her lips turned up in a smile.

"Now, Uncle Goofy, you need a dress."

Did he just hear her right? Him, in a dress? No way! "Hannah, I don't think—"

"A dress would be perfect," Emily interrupted.

Geoffrey gave her the evil eye. She was enjoying this too much.

"A dress ..." Hannah rummaged through the box.

Geoffrey's shoulders relaxed. There was no way he would fit into a dress that came from *that* box.

"I know where it is!" Hannah said. She got up and ran to a closet that Geoffrey hadn't noticed.

His heart sank. This might just happen. How was he going to get himself out of this?

"Found it! Miss Emily, help me."

"Help coming right up." Emily got up and raced to the closet.

Geoffrey looked at the door. Was there any way he could make it out in record time?

"Don't even think about it," Emily said. She was now holding up a green ball gown that might have been donated by a certain Spinster Heather from her Victorian cosplay collection.

Geoffrey grimaced. There was no way he was getting into that gown.

"Take it," Emily said.

"You're kidding," he whispered back.

"It's what you signed up for." She hid a smile.

"Uncle Goofy, do you like the princess

gown?" Hannah asked as she skipped back to where he sat.

"It's nice." What else could he say?

Emily held out the gown. Geoffrey let out a sigh and then accepted it.

"You can wear it over your T-shirt," she said.

"Of course, or were you expecting me to remove the shirt?" he whispered. He watched Emily's face turn a crimson red. "Emily, you have a naughty mind," he teased. Geoffrey never thought it would be possible, but Emily's face turned redder than before.

"Why is your face red, Miss Emily?" Hannah asked, her head cocked to the side.

Geoffrey chuckled. Emily deserved that—let her squirm for a change.

"Oh, it's nothing," she reassured Hannah. But she gave Geoffrey an evil look instead.

Geoffrey laughed. *That's what you get for making me wear this gown.*

"Uncle Goofy, be serious," Hannah scolded.

Geoffrey managed to look contrite. "Sorry, Hannah." He slipped the gown over his head. It was a loose fit, and he was certain he looked like a buffoon in it. The tiara got knocked off in the process, and he placed it right back on his head.

Hannah nodded as if pleased with her creation.

"Say cheese." Geoffrey turned too late to see Emily snap a picture of him with her phone.

"Give me that," he said.

"No."

He got up. "Don't make me come after you for it."

"You could try," Emily said taking one backward step after another.

"Uncle Goofy!"

He turned to Hannah. "What is it, kiddo?"

"It's time for princess tea."

Emily bellowed out a laugh, while Geoffrey had no choice but to sit down. Queen Hannah was taking no nonsense.

He accepted the tiny cup and saucer from her and pretended to sip the tea. It felt so ridiculous, but he continued with it for one reason only.

The joy on Hannah's face was worth everything.

~

Geoffrey stood up. He'd played princess with Hannah and Emily for a while but stopped once Hannah became sleepy. The princess box was packed up, and the dress returned to the closet.

"It's time for me to leave," Geoffrey said. "Hannah, I'll see you again next week, alright?"

"Bye, Uncle Goofy." She gave him a hug. "Thank you for being a good princess," she whispered. Then she yawned.

"My pleasure, kiddo."

He let her go, winked at Emily, and left the house.

Geoffrey entered his SUV and leaned his head against the headrest.

This had been the weirdest morning he'd ever had, but it was also the most fun. He'd enjoyed the interaction with both Emily and Hannah, and it had reminded him of how it could very easily have been him and a family of his own.

His phone pinged, and he looked at the screen. It was a text message from Emily.

Emily: You look cute, and I thought you might like a copy.

Geoffrey grinned as he stared at the picture

she'd sent. He did look cute, contrary to what he'd assumed earlier.

Another text came in.

Emily: Don't worry, it's only for my viewing pleasure. I'll keep it safe.

He chuckled. She'd better. He still had a public reputation to maintain.

Geoffrey: Thanks. I'll hold you to it.

Geoffrey dropped the phone back in the car's cup holder.

He'd always been content with his life, but now Emily was making him yearn for things he'd never known he wanted. This wasn't good, especially with someone he knew so little of.

But he had a feeling this was one train he couldn't stop.

CHAPTER 24

*E*mily watched Geoffrey leave, her cheeks still warm from seeing the wink. She felt a tug on her sleeve, and looked down.

"Miss Emily?" Hannah said.

"Yes, Hannah?"

"Do you like Uncle Goofy?"

Emily's eyes widened. How did this kid sense what she wasn't even sure of herself? "Why do you ask?"

Hannah gave Emily a toothy grin. "I like Uncle Goofy," she said with a wistful tone in her voice. "I wish he was my daddy."

"Oh, honey." Emily bent down and gathered Hannah into her arms. Well, that said everything. Hannah, though cheerful and always kind, didn't just take to anyone.

"It's okay," Hannah said in a cheerful tone. "He's still my Uncle Goofy."

Kids. Very resilient. This was another reason why she adored them so much.

Emily had to admit that the thought of Geoffrey as someone's daddy sat really well with her. Anyone who could answer to 'Uncle Goofy' with a smile on his face was a rockstar in her book. And it didn't seem such a bad idea if she was included in that setup.

Okay, time to end the daydream. Which was all it could ever be in her life given how much baggage she had. Emily also had a little princess that needed her sleep.

She gave Hannah a kiss on the cheek. "Let's go take a nap."

But she couldn't help but look forward to Friday when she'd see Geoffrey again.

CHAPTER 25

*E*mily stood in the event center the following week and surveyed the area. The decorations were now complete, and the center was ready for the next day's event.

It looked whimsical and ethereal, like a Christmas wonderland, and it had turned out better than she would have imagined it, from the candy cane runway where folks could take pictures as they arrived to the story reading grove where Santa would read to the children. Emily could already tell that the inflatable snow globe photo area would be a hit.

"It looks fantastic," said the now familiar voice that made her skin hum. Emily glanced at

Geoffrey—she hadn't noticed when he'd reached her side.

"Everyone worked hard to make it a reality," she responded.

"But we had a good leader," he countered.

It felt good to hear him say that, but Emily said nothing.

Geoffrey glanced at her. "It's really not hard to say thanks for the compliment."

Emily smiled. How would he have known that she hadn't received praise in years until about a year ago and was still unaccustomed to accepting them? Besides, it had really been a team effort. "Thank you," she said simply.

"Would you like to grab some coffee?" he asked.

Emily felt a tendril of excitement wrap around her heart. She hadn't really expected Geoffrey to ask her out again—she'd assumed he only said that last week for courtesy's sake. She'd planned to go home and rest after a busy workweek at her new job.

But a part of her didn't want to pass up this opportunity to get to know him better.

"Okay," she said.

Emily sat opposite Geoffrey at the same coffee shop they'd been in last week. The small space had acquired a more festive mood with all the Christmas trimmings and decorations. Even the staff were not left out with their cute Christmas hats.

"I figured you might want to stay close," Geoffrey said. "But I could take you to a better place for coffee if that's what you'd prefer."

It was as if he'd read her mind. One score in his favor. "This is fine, thank you," she responded.

The waitress, who had taken their order as soon as they arrived, returned with two steaming cups of expresso.

"Thank you," Geoffrey said to her.

"You're welcome," the gorgeous brunette said as she placed the cup in front of him, gave him a sweet smile, and left.

Geoffrey lifted his cup to take a sip, and that was when Emily saw the note sticking out from under the saucer.

"I think she left you a note," Emily said, pointing to it.

"Okay." Geoffrey continued sipping his coffee.

"Aren't you going to take a look at it?" Emily asked.

"I know what it says."

Emily arched her eyebrow. "How? Do you know her?" She had to admit she felt a twinge of jealousy at the thought, which was strange considering they had nothing between them.

"It's always the same. Someone interested in a relationship."

"Oh, you're insufferable."

Geoffrey set down his cup. "What would you have me do? Send her a note?"

"You could at least read it."

"Do you realize it's worse if she sees me reading it and then doesn't get any kind of response from me? With this, she may think I didn't see the note, which is kinder."

What he said made a little sense, though she still thought it was rude to ignore the note.

"Don't judge me, Emily. This is something I've dealt with a lot. It's better for her to not entertain any hopes than to let her believe she has a chance and then crush it."

Was he now a mind reader? Anyway, it was best to keep her nose out of it. It wasn't really her business in the first place. It would have been different if they were dating.

She took a sip of her coffee. Now why was she thinking about this?

"Emily, would you be my date tomorrow?"

Emily almost choked on her drink. How did he know what just crossed her mind?

"Are you okay?" Geoffrey asked with a concerned look. "Do you need anything? Water?"

She waved him away. "I'm fine." But he looked unconvinced by her words. "I'm fine, seriously," she reiterated.

He relaxed his gaze. "So would you be my date at the Christmas festival tomorrow?"

"Why?" she asked.

"What do you mean?"

"You barely know me, and I'm sure there are tons of ladies lining up to go with you."

"I'm only interested in you."

Emily's heart skipped a bit. Did he have to be so direct?

"You shouldn't say such things," she said. "It

could turn my head and make me think you're serious." He had to be joking, right? She took another sip of her coffee.

"What if I mean it?" he said, the pull of his warm brown eyes tugging on her heartstrings.

No way. Yes, she was working on her confidence and appreciating her self-worth, but frankly, she didn't really have much going on for her. Besides, she wasn't ready for a relationship. She was only just beginning to find herself again, and that was the most important thing in her life right now.

In addition, wouldn't seeing them together set the rumor mill in motion? She was the new girl in town, and she didn't need any enemies.

Yet in spite of all the good reasons not to, she wanted to spend more time with Geoffrey. She liked who she was around him, and besides, going to the festival alone would truly suck. Was it so bad if she wanted to enjoy this little slice of happiness for a change? There was nothing wrong with spending time together as just friends.

"Okay, I'll hang out with you," she said.

"If that's what you are calling it," Geoffrey said with a bemused smile.

Emily took another sip of her coffee.

Hopefully, she hadn't just made a mistake.

CHAPTER 26

Geoffrey took one more look at himself in his grey military-style coat over a blue button-down shirt and a pair of blue jeans. He looked good, if he said so himself, but that didn't stop him from being nervous about his date with Emily at the Christmas fair, though of course he was excited about it. Maybe a pep talk with Phillip might help.

Geoffrey headed in the direction of Phillip's office and knocked on the door. Hearing a faint response, he entered and shut the door behind him. "Sir—"

"Thank goodness you're here, Geoffrey," a voice said from the large screen on the wall.

"Could you help me convince Philip to make an investment in SechMed?"

Oops. He hadn't expected Bori to be on-screen. Bori was Phillip's best friend and business partner, a healthcare stock investor who lived in California with his lovely wife, Annie. Geoffrey had forgotten that today was their weekly conference call via live video. "Hello, Bori."

"Leave Geoffrey out of this," Phillip said.

"Why?" Bori asked. "I'm pretty sure he's already made a decision about it, unlike you."

"Because Geoffrey is pretty busy these days."

Bori looked from Phillip to Geoffrey. "What is it? Tell me."

"I have no idea what Mr. Dexington is talking about," Geoffrey said.

"Whoa! What happened to your hair, Geoffrey?" Bori asked.

Geoffrey's ears heated. Why did Bori have to notice? It wasn't that very different from his usual style, was it?

"I like it," Bori continued. "It's different."

"Just trying something new," Geoffrey muttered.

"It suits you," Phillip said. "Makes you look younger."

"Why do I get the feeling you're laughing at me?" Geoffrey said.

"Why would I?" Phillip said with a twinkle in his eye. "I'm sure your lovely lady will like it."

"What lady?" Bori asked.

"Didn't you get the memo?" Phillip said.

What was Phillip talking about?

Bori looked from Geoffrey to Phillip. "What memo? Phillip, you've been holding out on me."

"Mother is just waiting for Geoffrey to make a move before she sweeps in," Phillip said. "If he's not careful, she might take matters into her own hands. And you don't want that, do you, Geoffrey?"

"I have to go," Geoffrey said, his ears burning by now. It had been a mistake to look for Phillip.

"Don't worry, Geoffrey," Phillip said. "We are on the sidelines cheering for you."

"Hey, guys, tell me what's going on," Geoffrey heard Bori say as he left the office. He could hear Phillip's laughter as he shut the door behind him.

Tease all you want, Phillip. Who knows? It might be Philip's turn this Christmas to meet the love of his life. And then guess who would be having a good time at his expense?

But first, Geoffrey was going to kill his hairdresser for suggesting this hair style to him.

Geoffrey spied her standing next to Santa as he read a Christmas story to the children gathered around him. He almost didn't recognize her—she had let down her hair for a change and looked stunning in a loose flowery top over blue jeans, her cream coat slung over her arm.

The event center was teeming with people with activities going full speed in different corners of the hall. It took a little time, but eventually Geoffrey made his way across the room till he was standing a few feet away from her.

She looked up at that moment, and her eyes lit up when they met his.

Geoffrey's heart skipped a beat. How was she able to elicit such a strong response from him? Yes, she was beautiful, but it was something within her that drew him to her like a moth to flame.

He gave her a smile in return. She moved from where she stood till she got to his side. "Hello," she said.

"Hi, Emily. You look fantastic."

"You too. I love the hair. It suits you."

"I aim to impress." Thank goodness she'd liked it.

She laughed, the lyrical notes tickling his senses. "Can't you be a bit modest?"

He chuckled. She had a way of making him feel at ease around her. "So shall we?" he said extending an elbow to her.

She hesitated for a moment, then she took it, and he tucked her arm in his, which felt so natural like it belonged there.

"So where are we starting?" she asked.

"Where would you like us to start?"

"Why don't we start with the candy cane runway?"

"Great idea."

That was the beginning of a wonderful afternoon. Geoffrey couldn't believe it was the same Emily that he had run into at the boutique. She was like a kid in a candy store, and he soon got caught up in her infectious joy. This was the first Christmas event he'd enjoyed in a long time, and he knew it was because of her. By the time they arrived at the snow globe photo booth, he'd realized he just wanted to be with her, get to know her, and never let go.

They took the last silly photo at the booth, and Geoffrey turned to her. "Emily …"

She turned to him, a smile on her face. "What is it? Are we done?"

"Would you go out with me?"

"For coffee? Sure."

This wasn't going as he thought it would.

Geoffrey swallowed. "I mean, would you go out with me as my girlfriend?"

CHAPTER 27

Emily's stomach twisted into a coil. Girlfriend? She wasn't ready to be tied to anyone yet! All she wanted from Geoffrey was to enjoy their friendship and see where it led them. "Are you sure?" she asked. "You barely know me. I don't even know how old you are."

"I'm forty-three."

Emily's eyes widened. "You look younger than your age."

"Does it bother you?" Geoffrey asked.

"No. My parents were seventeen years apart in age, and they had a great marriage before he died. I'm thirty-three, by the way."

"The gap doesn't bother me either. We can

take it as slow as you like, starting off as friends and going from there. I just want to make it clear to others that we're exclusive. I'm not asking you to marry me tomorrow or anything like that."

Her shoulders relaxed. It had been the right thing for him to say. "So exclusive friends?"

"Yes, but it could be much more than that if we like."

A part of her wanted to say no because of the burden of her past. She wasn't sure any sane man could handle it.

But there was something about Geoffrey she couldn't resist. Like she would be making the worst mistake of her life if she didn't take this chance, especially since he seemed ready to go at her pace.

She studied his face for a moment, and then took a deep breath and let it out. It was time to step out in faith. "Yes, I would like that," she said.

The joy that spread over Geoffrey's face was one Emily would remember for a long time. "Woohoo!" he shouted and lifted her in his arms.

"Put me down," Emily whispered, her face

and neck heating up, though she couldn't help smiling.

"Sorry." He set her down gently.

"You really mean it about taking it slow, right?" Emily asked.

"Yes. For as long as you like."

Emily felt peace in her heart at his words. She would get to know him better, and he would get the chance to meet who she truly was. If it worked out, then she would tell him about her past.

CHAPTER 28

FOUR MONTHS LATER

*E*mily crossed and uncrossed her legs as she waited in her apartment for Geoffrey to pick her up. Hannah had a piano recital in New York, and both Geoffrey and Emily had been invited. Emily had wondered how they would get there, but Geoffrey had hinted it was a surprise.

But more importantly, Emily had decided today was a special day, a new beginning of some sort for their relationship. She was excited for Geoffrey to get here.

The doorbell chimed, and Emily hurried over to look through the peephole.

It was Geoffrey.

She flung the door open and gave him a warm smile. "Hello!"

"Wow, you look stunning!" Geoffrey said.

Emily beamed. She'd seen the yellow long-sleeved floor-length gown with a fitted waist in a dress shop and had fallen in love with it. It had taken courage to wear it, but Geoffrey had always been proud of her in her baggy clothes, and since she was more comfortable in her skin now, Emily wanted to please Geoffrey for a change. "Thank you," she said. "You look nice too." And he did in his custom black tuxedo with his top hair slicked back into a man bun.

Geoffrey entered and shut the door behind him. "You know you look great no matter what you wear," he said.

See? This was why she loved this man. Wait, did the L word just come to mind? Emily gasped. This was a big deal, and something to think about.

"Are you okay?" Geoffrey asked, concern written all over his face.

"I'm fine." She gave him a warm smile. "I think we should start going. By the way, how are we getting to New York?"

"We'll be taking the jet. It belongs to the

Dexingtons, but I'm allowed to use it as a family member. I don't really travel much, so I don't need one of my own."

Emily chuckled. "Like you could afford it."

Geoffrey looked at her with serious eyes. "I can."

"Stop joking, Geoffrey. A jet would cost A LOT of money."

"I know. I can afford it."

Emily laughed. "It's fine, Geoffrey, really."

"But if I was a billionaire, would it bother you?"

"Well, no … yes."

A lazy smile teased his lips. "Which is it?"

"No, because I've had a chance to know you without it, and yes, because it would make me realize you're way out of my league."

"I would still be the same old Geoffrey. The money wouldn't define me."

"You're not old."

"You should tell Mrs. Dexington that."

Emily chuckled. "She's still on your case?" Emily had met Helen and Alex Dexington at Phillip's wedding when Geoffrey had introduced her to them. Alex had offered her a job at Dexington Healthcare, but Emily had declined the offer, choosing instead to stay at the Christmas farm. She loved her job there, and Steve had recently promoted her to the marketing manager position, insisting the apartment came with the role.

"Every day now, since she found out about you," Geoffrey said. "If she had her way, I'd be getting married tomorrow."

"Well, that's not going to happen. Unless you find someone else."

"Are you rejecting the position?" Geoffrey said with a tease in his voice.

"I don't know. You have to ask again in a few months to find out."

"Ouch! That hurts."

Emily leaned forward and gave him a kiss on the cheek. "Does it feel better now?"

"Not really. I need another kiss to confirm."

She moved in to give him another peck, but Geoffrey turned his face, and the kiss landed on his lips instead. "You sneaky little thing!" Emily exclaimed.

"Little thing?" Before she could move away, his arms wrapped around her. "Now, you have to be punished."

Emily laughed. "Let me go."

"I will after you serve your punishment."

"Which is what?"

"A big old kiss on these charming lips."

"Talk about being vain. Your lips are charming?"

Geoffrey gave her a wink. "You know they are. I've seen you staring at them."

Emily's face grew hot. "Has anyone told you you're incorrigible?"

"A few times. Okay, I'm still waiting. You have to be quick, otherwise I might add a little something to it."

"Like what?"

"A tickling session might be in order."

"No, you won't." Emily was ticklish—Geoffrey had found out a couple weeks ago.

"You want to bet?"

"Okay, okay, I'll do it."

Then Emily leaned forward and planted a kiss on those lips that had called out to her since forever. The butterflies in her belly began to stir, and her skin tingled with excitement. He tasted sweet like chocolate and mint, like the essence of all things pure and new, and she wanted more. Emily looped her arms around his neck, deepening the kiss, his clean fresh scent enveloping her.

Then Geoffrey kissed her back, a sweet cadence of soft gentle kisses and hard breath-stealing ones, and Emily realized at that moment what she had been missing out on and how much Geoffrey had been holding back. The butterflies in her belly danced and went into overdrive. Her skin tingled with sparks of electricity as his hands wove into her hair and cupped the back of her head.

And then he called her name in the gentle way that was uniquely his as he continued to kiss her, and her senses exploded. It was like an avalanche of love and sweetness rolled over her, and Emily basked in them.

Geoffrey eventually broke the kiss and leaned his forehead against hers.

"Thank you for being brave," he said.

"Thank you for helping," Emily responded. "I knew you were teasing to make it easier for me." Emily had asked to take things slow in the relationship, and Geoffrey had acquiesced without asking questions. But she'd known today that she wanted to kiss him for the first time, and Geoffrey must have sensed it. She adored this man of hers that understood her.

"Okay, let's get going," Geoffrey said.

"Are you sure you don't want second help-ings?" Emily asked as her face and neck grew hot.

Geoffrey chuckled. "You have no idea how much I'd love to, but I'm afraid we'd never leave this apartment today if I did."

"I think the exit is this way," Emily said, picking up her purse and hurrying toward the door to avoid Geoffrey seeing how tomato-red her face had turned at his words.

Geoffrey laughed and followed her out.

The ride to New York was magical, and the red carpet treatment at Carnegie Hall was one Emily would never forget. But the best part of the evening was when Hannah got on stage in her cute little black frock and sat down to play.

Emily had no idea she had a budding pianist on her hands. Hannah played with a ferocious-ness and then softness that belied her age, and the whole hall gave her a standing ovation when she was done.

Emily wiped the tears from her eyes. She was

super proud of Hannah and honored that she'd witnessed this moment.

She rushed backstage with Geoffrey following her till she saw Hannah standing away from the other young performers and looking around. Her face lit up with delight as soon as her eyes fell on Emily and Geoffrey.

"You came!" she said and ran into Emily's arms.

Emily kissed the top of her head. "You were so good," she said. "You made me cry, and I'm so proud of you."

"You did great, kiddo," Geoffrey chimed in and gave her a bouquet of flowers.

"Thank you." Hannah gave him a hug in return.

"Where's Martha?" Geoffrey asked. Martha had escorted Hannah to New York for the event, and they'd met her briefly before the recital began.

"Oscar was sick," Hannah said. Oscar was the other kid from the orphanage that had been billed to play as well.

Emily's phone buzzed, and she checked the screen. It was a text message from Martha, saying she'd taken Oscar to the ER. He was better, but needed to stay a few more hours before they could discharge him. So could Emily and Geoffrey take Hannah back to Dexington?

"What is it?" Geoffrey asked. Emily showed him the text message. "That's fine. I'll make sure the jet comes back to pick them up when they're ready."

"Okay, I'll let her know." Emily typed a response and then tucked the phone into her purse.

"Miss Emily?" Hannah said.

"Yes, Hannah?"

"I'm tired. Could we go home now?"

"Sure."

As they turned to leave, an elderly lady in a black lace dress approached them and handed Hannah another bouquet of flowers. "I just wanted to say thank you for playing so beautifully, little lady," she said to Hannah.

Hannah giggled and curtsied.

The woman smiled in return, and then turned to Emily. "Is she yours?" she asked.

Emily was at a loss for words. How would she introduce their relationship without creating an awkward situation for Hannah?

"We're her family," Geoffrey said.

That was it—Geoffrey had described their relationship perfectly.

And Emily realized she liked the sound of it very much.

CHAPTER 29

Emily put the finishing touches to her makeup and leaned back. She usually only used lip gloss and some blush, but today was different—it was going to be a memorable day in her life no matter what the outcome was.

She smiled at her reflection. The lady in front of her had come a long way from the one who'd lost hope that anything good could happen in her life. She'd found herself, and love from the most wonderful man in the world had done the rest.

What a difference a good man could make, which was why Emily had finally found the strength to open up fully about her past.

She'd wanted to tell Geoffrey her story many

times over the last few months, but a cowardly part of her had been afraid and wanted to hold on to this bit of happiness—that she'd been missing for much of her adult life—for just a little longer. Though she'd hinted at her past as her relationship with Geoffrey had grown, she'd lacked the courage to share the full details.

Then Emily discovered he was going to propose soon, and she realized it was time. So when Geoffrey invited her for dinner, Emily decided she would take the bull by the horns. She had to let him know before he popped the question. Proposing to her was a choice he could only make after seeing her fully for who she was. So she'd told Geoffrey she had something to say to him tonight.

She looked at the clock on the wall. Geoffrey was due to arrive in the next ten minutes. Her heart blossomed with joy at the thought of seeing him again, despite how anxious she was about everything.

The shrill sound of her phone rent the air.

She picked it up and looked at the screen. It was an unknown number, though it had a Dexington prefix. Who could it be? Maybe it was Nancy—she'd mentioned that her parents were adding a new number to the dry cleaning business.

Emily swiped the answer button. "Hello?" she said.

"Leanne Ashton."

Emily's heart pounded. The combination of the voice and a name she'd considered long dead brought a feeling of dread over her.

"Who is it?" she managed to croak out.

The voice gave a maniacal chuckle. "You don't remember me? I've been looking for you for a long time."

Emily's mind raced as fear worked its way through her body. The voice sounded so much like Calvin's, but it couldn't be. Calvin was dead and buried six feet under. Then she remembered the only other person that was crazy enough to hunt her down. But his voice didn't sound like this. Or had it changed? "Billy?" she ventured.

The voice laughed. "The one and the same. You really thought you could disappear after killing my brother. You had it all planned, didn't you?"

Fear crept into Emily's heart and squeezed it tight. Most folks had assumed that Calvin was the vicious one, but Emily had known better.

Underneath Billy's genteel manner hid a vicious snake.

But she was no longer the young woman who used to cower in fear despite the violence against her. She took a deep breath and exhaled. "What do you want?" she said in a quiet controlled voice though her hands trembled.

"I want a hundred thousand dollars, otherwise I'm going to tell everyone in your new town what a murderer you are. You know how that would end."

Was he insane? "I don't have that kind of money!"

"Well, you have to find it, one way or the other. You can sell your body if necessary. It won't be a stretch considering."

Fury rose in Emily's heart. How dare he? Calvin had beaten her black and blue and left her almost dead when she refused to have sex with his friends after collecting money over her head from them, but she'd decided at the time that it was better to die than lose her final shred of dignity. Now his brother thought he could continue where Calvin had stopped. She would die before she let that happen. "I have no money for you, Billy. Even if I did, I would never give it to you."

She heard his ragged breath over the phone as he struggled to rein in his anger. *He must be pretty desperate if he was making the effort*, she concluded. "You have one week, Leanne. If I don't see the money by then, I'll make sure you lose *everything*. One week. That's all you have." Then he chuckled. "Sleep tight, my pretty little Leanne." The line went dead.

Emily's body shook from head to toe. She'd hated every moment Calvin had called her that. Emily was tempted to crush the phone to destroy any connection with this evil from the past. But it wouldn't solve the problem.

Then she remembered Geoffrey was arriving shortly.

What was she going to do?

CHAPTER 30

"Emily Roth, will you marry me?" Geoffrey asked, while on one knee as he held out a beautiful diamond ring resting in a black velvet box to her.

He'd been looking forward to this moment for many months now. Their relationship had grown by leaps and bounds after the New York event, and Geoffrey had fallen in love with her more and more each day, eventually realizing Emily Roth was the one for him.

Geoffrey gazed into her tear-filled brown eyes, and then reached out to brush away the single tear that streaked down her cheek. "Will you do me the honor of being my wife?" he asked. "I promise to love and cherish you all the days of my life." They had just finished a candlelight dinner in Emily's favorite restaurant. Geoffrey had hired out the whole place for the occasion.

He waited with bated breath. It was a risk proposing to her during Christmas time—anyone he'd ever loved had always left him during this one season most people looked forward to. But Emily had showed up in his life during last year's Christmas season, changing what had always been a time of heartache for him, and he hoped proposing to her during Christmas would continue the good streak.

"No," Emily responded in a soft voice.

Geoffrey's breath caught, and his heart rate quickened. Had he heard right? In the past few weeks, he'd given enough hints that he planned to pop the question soon, and she'd seemed excited about it.

He blinked rapidly. No, he'd probably misunderstood what she meant.

"I'm sorry, Geoffrey. I can't marry you," Emily said in a choked voice.

Geoffrey's heart sank. She was really saying

no. He got up from his bended knee and collapsed into his chair. But he didn't understand. "Why?" he asked, hurt at what he'd just heard.

Emily fidgeted in her seat as she clasped her hands together, refusing to meet his eye.

"Emily, please look at me," he said in a quiet voice.

Her beautiful blonde hair, cascading in waves around her face, moved with her as she shook her head. He noticed more tears were now running down her face, and his heart couldn't help twisting in pain at the sight. Geoffrey had never seen Emily so distraught. Why was she rejecting him if it hurt her so much? Something had to be wrong.

"I'm so sorry," she repeated. Then she snatched up her purse and coat from the chair beside her and ran out.

Geoffrey sat stunned for a moment. Then he rushed to his feet, leaving behind the half-eaten dinner. "Emily, wait!" As much as he still didn't understand what just happened, he had to make sure she was okay.

He hurried outside only to see Emily enter a

waiting cab, which then pulled away from the curb. "Emily!"

Emily stared straight ahead, and the cab kept going without stopping. Geoffrey scanned the area, but there were no other taxis available, and his car was still with the valet service. There was no way he could catch up with her in time.

He let out a sigh. Knowing Emily, it was best to give her some space tonight. So he watched helplessly as the cab raced down the driveway and soon disappeared from view.

Geoffrey ran his hands through his hair. The cold air beat against his skin, but he didn't notice. What had just happened? Had he read the signs all wrong? No, he didn't think so. If he'd offended her, Emily would have told him immediately as she'd always done. And if she'd never planned to marry him, she wouldn't have waited till now to let him know—Emily was not that kind of person —and she'd been fine as they chatted and laughed on the phone yesterday. It had to be something recent that had made her change her mind.

Geoffrey plodded back to his seat, collapsed in it, and loosened his tie. What could it be? He racked his brain, but nothing came to mind.

He rested his head in his hands. He had to pull himself together, but it was easier said than done. The rejection still stung no matter what had brought it on. It was like a large boulder with jagged edges had rolled over his heart and crushed it into a million pieces, and it hurt worse than when he'd lost his parents and his ex-girlfriend.

Geoffrey straightened and sucked in a deep breath. Something told him Emily still loved him, and it wasn't time to give up yet. He still had a chance. He'd accepted the pain in times past because he'd had no choice, but this time was different.

Geoffrey stood. It wasn't over yet. He was going to find out the truth no matter what it took and beat this Christmas jinx.

Because Emily was worth fighting for.

Geoffrey walked into Dexington House and through the large foyer. The lights were still on in the living room, but he wasn't surprised. Helen had known he was proposing tonight and was probably waiting up for him.

And he was right. She sat on the main couch reading a book, looking regal as always in a grey silk blouse paired with cream loose pants. Unlike what folks knew of her, Helen was one of the most well-read people that Geoffrey had ever met. Even though Alex Dexington was the face of the Dexington Healthcare conglomerate, Helen was more than half of the brains behind it. But she preferred to work behind the scenes, despite how many times Alex had requested otherwise.

She looked up as he entered. "Well, did she accept?" she asked. Geoffrey could always trust Helen to cut to the chase. "Spill."

Geoffrey sank into the chair opposite hers and said nothing.

Helen closed the book and sat up. "Oh dear, this must be serious. What happened?"

'She said no."

"No? Why?"

"That's it. I don't know why. But she was very upset and left immediately."

Helen leaned back. "That's weird. Emily is such a sweet and nice girl. Something must be wrong. Did anything happen recently?"

Geoffrey ran his hand through his hair. "I

don't think so. Or maybe I missed the signs."

Helen leaned forward. "Geoffrey, I know you're disappointed, but I don't want you to give up. Unless she is a fantastic actress, that girl loves you. Of that I'm very certain. Something or someone must be scaring her enough to make her turn you down."

Hope flickered in Geoffrey's heart. He'd figured something was wrong, but hearing Helen validate it meant he was on the right path.

"So what do you plan to do?" Helen asked.

"I'll give her some space, then I plan to see her to find out what's wrong. Hopefully, she'll open up to me."

"Don't wait too long, okay?"

"I won't."

"I'm sure you'll prefer to handle everything yourself, but let me know if there's any way I can help," Helen said. It must have taken an effort for Helen to hold back from intervening. "And don't worry, your secret is safe with me. I'll hold off from letting Phillip and Sarah know." Sarah was Philip's wife, and they had gotten married earlier in the year. "Alex is going to find out, but you can trust his silence. Everything is going to turn out just fine."

"Thank you."

"Alright, go on."

Geoffrey got up and headed to the exit that led in the direction of his property.

He would give Emily a day.

Then he was going to find out the truth.

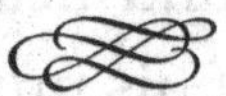

CHAPTER 31

*E*mily made a funny face at Hannah as she rinsed the soap off the little girl's body. She'd arrived early, as usual, at the orphanage to help with bathing the little ones.

Hannah giggled and splashed the water in the bathtub, spilling it all over Emily.

Emily gave her a small smile. Thank goodness she was wearing a waterproof apron, otherwise she would have to go home and change her clothes before heading in for work. She loved volunteering at the orphanage, and it always helped to ease the pain that lay buried deep in her heart. But today, it couldn't change how terrible she felt for what she had done last night.

She'd hurt Geoffrey. Emily had seen the pain

in her heart mirrored in his eyes last night. What should have been the most wonderful day in their lives had turned to disaster instead.

It was all her fault. She'd known that Geoffrey would propose soon. Over the past year, she'd seen firsthand what a wonderful, selfless, and good man Geoffrey was.

He treated her like an equal partner in the relationship—all her thoughts and feelings mattered to him. He sought out her opinions and encouraged her to try out anything he sensed she was interested in. A part of her had always believed she was worthy of love, but seeing it mirrored every day in his words and actions had been beyond her expectations.

But she hadn't known he was going to propose yesterday. Geoffrey had invited her out for dinner as usual, and Emily had no idea it was going to be any different. So she'd only planned to use the opportunity to tell him about her past.

But then her phone rang, and everything changed.

She'd thought her past was over. Done, dead, and buried. Emily had left everything behind in New Jersey and had come to Dexington to start afresh. She'd thought she succeeded, but she must have been fooling herself. The evil from her past had arisen from the ashes and come back to haunt her last night. The one voice she'd never thought to hear again had found her.

She'd still been in shock from the phone call when the proposal had popped out of left field. Emily knew right then there was no way she was going to drag this sweet man into this nightmare. Geoffrey was too good to be tainted and hurt by her darkness.

Accepting his proposal would have meant dragging him into the mess that used to be her life, and that was something she would never allow. She had to keep him safe and away from the evil in her past that didn't want to let her go. If Billy found out about Geoffrey, he would do everything out of jealousy to destroy him, since he represented happiness to Emily, something his brother Calvin had never been able to give.

So as much as it broke her heart, she'd had no choice but to force out the words to reject his offer to love and cherish her forever.

Because it was the only way to protect him, even though it was a decision she was sure to regret for the rest of her life. It didn't solve her problem with Billy, but it would keep Geoffrey, her loved one, safe. Which was something she'd failed at in times past.

"Miss Emily?" Hannah asked, bringing Emily back to the present.

Emily picked up the towel from its hook, dried off Hannah's wet blonde hair, and wrapped the towel around her. "Yes, sweetie?"

"Are you crying?"

Emily wiped a hand across her cheek and felt the wetness of a tear. She didn't even know when it had happened. She forced a smile at Hannah. "I'm fine."

Hannah leaned forward and wrapped her little arms around Emily. "Hugs make every-thing better."

Emily chuckled, and she felt her spirits lift. Somehow, Hannah had known Emily needed a hug today. "Thank you, Hannah."

"You're welcome," the little girl said.

Then Hannah's stomach rumbled. Her face turned red, and she grinned sheepishly.

Emily tweaked Hannah's nose and laughed. "I guess I need to get you to the kitchen ASAP!" She lifted Hannah from the bathtub and carried her into the room to help her dress up.

It was no use crying over spilled milk. Emily had to put what had happened yesterday behind her and take each day at a time, no matter how empty her life felt without Geoffrey.

Because that was all she had now.

Emily forced one foot in front of the other as she made her way to the door of her apartment at the Christmas tree farm. It had been a rough day at work, and Emily knew why.

She missed Geoffrey. It was like a big hole had been carved in her heart, and her body felt heavy as lead. How was she going to function for the next few days or weeks if she could barely get through today?

"Hello, Emily."

Her head jerked in the direction of the voice, only to see the man she'd missed all day standing in front of her. A warmth spread through her heart as she watched him straighten from the wall he'd been leaning on, but the look of worry and pain in his eyes almost made her break down.

He didn't deserve this, and she could see her

rejection was killing him. And in that moment, Emily knew she had to tell him the truth.

"Come in," she said wearily.

She entered the apartment, knowing he would follow her in. She dropped her bag on the coffee table and sank into the couch. Geoffrey took the seat opposite her.

"Are you okay?" he asked.

Tears sprang to Emily's eyes. He should be mad that she'd turned down his proposal, yet here he was concerned about her wellbeing. This was why she was unworthy of him, the reason she didn't want the darkness from her past to destroy him. He was all light and hope and the best things in this world.

But she would tell him the truth even if it meant he would turn away from her. Emily wouldn't blame him if he did, and she would still cherish the time they'd had together. "There's something I need to tell you …"

Emily told him about the devil she got married to at eighteen years of age. She'd met him as she worked in a convenience store trying to save up money to go to college. She and her mom had fallen on hard times after her dad died but had scrimped and saved to meet their needs.

Emily had aced high school and had acquired some college credits by the time she graduated. But her mom had been diagnosed with Alzheimer's disease, and whatever little money Emily had saved for college had gone to her treatment and care.

"He swept me off my feet, got my mom into a really good facility, and promised me I would attend college after we were married," Emily said. "I was so naive that I believed him."

Geoffrey said nothing, but Emily could see he was listening. "Everything was fine for the first few weeks after marriage, and then Calvin began to beat me. Nothing I did was ever good enough for him. I called the cops after the first time, but it only backfired. No one believed me. Instead, they said it was all my fault. After all, he was a police officer and could do no wrong."

She took a tremulous breath as she paused. She hadn't realized the depth of pain and despair that recalling the memories would bring. "Calvin threatened to kill my mom if I ever reported him again. She was the most precious person to me, and I couldn't take the chance that he would harm her. So I stayed."

Emily got up and walked over to the

window. It wasn't dark yet, and a slight breeze swayed the trees. Geoffrey stayed seated and didn't move. "It got worse after that. Every day was a living hell. Then he came home drunk one afternoon. I'd been very tired and had decided to take a nap, not expecting him to be back at that time. He barged into the bedroom and began to beat me as usual. And what was my crime this time?" Emily gave a bitter laugh. "Leaving the toilet seat down instead of up."

She felt a hand on her shoulder to see Geoffrey standing beside her. Emily turned back to the window. She couldn't look at Geoffrey—it was the only way she could finish her story in one piece. "I escaped into the hallway, but he managed to grab me before I could make it down the stairs," she said. "Then he gripped my throat and began to squeeze the life from me."

Emily looked through the window and saw a bird flitting from one Christmas tree to another. How good it must feel to be so carefree. "I fought him as hard as I could and managed to loosen his hold," she said. "But then he pushed me down the stairs." She could remember how each part of her body had hurt as she bounced from one stair to the next.

"Unfortunately for Calvin, I managed to grab him along for the ride. When I woke up in the hospital later, I was told a neighbor had heard the commotion and found me lying unconscious at the bottom of the stairs with Calvin dead beside me."

Emily's mouth was dry, and she wished she had a glass of water. But getting it would distract her, and she needed to finish the story. "Considering how the cops had treated me before, I was surprised they closed the case as an accident. Unfortunately, the news of what happened to me reached my mom while she was lucid, and she went into shock and died."

She suddenly felt cold and wrapped her arms around herself. "I was like a zombie after my mom's death until Nancy came down to see me. We were close in high school, and someone must have called her to let her know what happened. She encouraged me to pack up my life, move to Dexington, and start all over again.

"I was able to apply to a local college with my college credits, and I buried myself in an intensive course load. It was the only way to deal with the grief and everything that had happened. Facing each new day gradually got easier, and then it was time to graduate before I knew it." Emily gave Geoffrey a small smile. "Then I met you.

"You were the best thing that ever happened to me," she continued. "I really thought my past was behind me. And when you hinted you were going to propose, I knew it was time to tell you the truth. That's what I had planned to do during the dinner. But then I got a call from Calvin's brother before you arrived. I have no idea how he found me, but he called and threatened to tell everyone in Dexington that I was a killer, if I didn't pay him off immediately.

"But I had no idea you were going to propose *yesterday*, so when you did, I didn't want you pulled into this mess, so that was why I turned you down," she said. "You deserve better."

CHAPTER 32

Geoffrey's head spun. This was the last thing he'd expected to hear. How could she have kept something like this from him? It was clear it wasn't her fault, but it was a lot to process now, and he needed a quiet place to do so. "I have to go," he said.

Emily's face fell, and he could see the despair written all over it. But if she thought he was abandoning her, then she didn't really know who he was.

Geoffrey gathered Emily into his arms. "I'll be back tomorrow," he said, planting a kiss on her head.

Then he released her and left the apartment.

CHAPTER 33

Emily locked the door behind Geoffrey and slid to the floor. Geoffrey had said he'd be back, but she knew better. What she'd shared was too much for anyone, and there was no doubt this was the end of the relationship between them.

Though she felt some release at finally telling him about her past, her heart felt hollow at the burden she'd placed on him. No one deserved that, him least of all.

She was sure he would never see her the same way again. Her hands were stained with blood and always would be. Geoffrey deserved a future with a woman without baggage that would weigh him down.

Emily's eyes brimmed with tears, but she refused to cry. It had been her fault for marrying a man like Calvin, and she could blame no one else for how her life had turned out.

It was all on her for losing a man as good as Geoffrey.

CHAPTER 34

Geoffrey stared at the file in front of him. It was worse than he'd thought. He'd called a private investigator he liked to use for Dexington Healthcare's official business soon after he left her place, and the man had gone to work immediately.

Twenty hours later, Geoffrey had the police report and copies of everything else about the case.

Her ex-husband had been a monster. What Emily had told him had only scratched the surface. She'd been battered multiple times and had been a regular visitor at the hospital, but no one had helped her. She had even lost a baby from the fall on the stairs, and it wasn't her first miscarriage. Geoffrey couldn't imagine how she must have felt.

Now he understood why she'd always expressed mixed feelings about having a baby whenever they talked about building a family, when it was obvious that she loved kids from the way she doted on Hannah. That alone would have been enough to break her.

How had she been able to bounce back? The Emily he'd met was a far cry from the one in the report—a lot of healing must have taken place in the months after.

Geoffrey had a newfound respect for her. It must have taken a lot of determination and grit to pull herself together and move forward beyond that horror, and she had done it.

There was no way Geoffrey would let the monster from her past win.

He got up and picked up his car keys.

He needed to see her.

CHAPTER 35

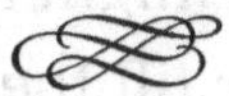

The knock on the door turned Emily's attention away from the window where she had been standing. She'd taken the day off from work, but had spent most of it in bed or staring out this window.

Her heart quickened. There was only one person who could get past the elevators to her door. The company had installed an access card reader to the penthouse after she had moved in.

She hurried to the door and swung it open. One minute Geoffrey was standing outside the threshold, and the next she was in his arms. It was exactly what Emily needed, and she let out a tremulous sigh.

"I'm so sorry," he said. That simple statement broke her, and all the heartache and pain flowed out through the tears she'd never allowed herself to shed since everything happened. She'd known at the time she would be lost if she did and might never recover.

Geoffrey held her till the tears stopped flowing, till she had nothing more to give. Then he led her to the couch and sat beside her.

Emily still couldn't believe he was here, sitting at her side. She'd never expected he would really come back. Who would after hearing her story and how broken she was? Even though she was stronger now, that didn't mean there weren't going to be moments when she would retreat to how she'd been before. And it could eventually wear down any man, no matter how patient and loving he was.

But he had come, and that alone was a miracle.

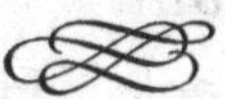

CHAPTER 36

"Tell me about him," Geoffrey said.

"About who?"

"The person who called you," he insisted.

"Oh. That's Calvin's brother, Billy."

"How much does he want?"

"Everything I have and more, so that he doesn't reveal my past here."

"Has he ever asked for money before?"

"No, probably because he couldn't find me. I changed my last name back to my maiden name and took my middle name as my first name."

"Emily suits you better," Geoffrey said.

She gave him a small smile. "I've always preferred it, and mom loved calling me that. So it seemed a good time as any to adopt the name."

Geoffrey reached out and swept a tendril of her hair away from her face. "Did he say when he would call you again?"

"In about a week. He's always had a gambling problem, so I assume he's in some sort of trouble. He must have blown through everything his brother had—I didn't want any of it and left everything behind."

"Do you have any pictures of him?"

"He should be in my wedding pictures, but I burnt them all. But I know his social media account. Give me one second."

Emily fished out her phone, scrolled through some pages, and then found his profile. "Here he is," she said and handed the phone to Geoffrey.

Geoffrey studied the face. "Don't worry, I'll take care of him," he said.

A look of concern crossed Emily's face. "Billy is dangerous. I don't want you getting entangled in his mess."

"Don't worry. I'm pretty sure he's broken the law multiple times and gotten away with it, given his brother was a cop. He won't even know what hit him. I'll make sure he stays away from you for good." He gave her a reassuring smile. "And I won't do anything stupid."

"I know you won't," she said quietly.

Geoffrey pulled her into his arms. This was where she belonged, and not even Billy could take her away from him. "Everything will be alright," he said, planting a kiss on her head. Emily snuggled deeper into his arms.

"I've missed you," he said.

"I've missed you too."

They stayed that way for a while. Then Geoffrey loosened his embrace and stared into her eyes. "I love you, Emily Roth, and I won't let anything happen to you."

She gave him a small smile in return.

Then Geoffrey bent his head and gave her a tender kiss on her soft lips, a kiss he hoped told her he was here to stay and wasn't going anywhere.

Then he reluctantly released her. "I have to go and take care of this," he said. "I'd like to do so before he reaches out to you again."

"Please be safe," she said.

Geoffrey gave Emily another hug and kissed her forehead. "I love you," he said.

Then he got up and left her apartment, his mind already formulating a plan.

He had a lot to do.

Billy would wish he'd never crossed his path.

Emily wrung her hands as she waited in her apartment. Geoffrey had given her a call a few hours ago that a warrant had gone out for Billy's arrest. Billy was a wild one, always had been, but he'd always been able to escape from the law through his brother's police connections. It was possible he would slip the net.

She paced the living room, but the air felt stifling, full of foreboding. Emily needed fresh air to clear her head. So she donned her coat and took the elevator to the building's lobby.

Emily stepped out into the cold night and inhaled. Definitely better, but she was still worried as she wrapped the coat tightly around her. She hoped Geoffrey was safe.

A hand grabbed her arm in a steely grip with another pressing a knife against her neck. A strong smell of onions and an unwashed body wafted up her nose, and Emily felt nauseated. "Don't move," a male voice said.

Fear froze in her veins. Billy had found her. Why hadn't it occurred to her that he would come looking for her?

Emily swallowed. She couldn't let the fear rule her. She had to find a way out. "What do you want?" she asked.

"You, whore. I've been watching your every move. You thought your new boy toy could save you. I looked into him, you know. A butler? Ha!" Billy gave a harsh chuckle. "I didn't expect you to sink so low after killing my brother. But something told me to dig deeper, and then I found out who he truly was—richer than the devil. No wonder you stuck to him. I knew there had to be a catch."

"I don't ..." Emily's mind swirled in confusion. What was Billy talking about? She knew Geoffrey had money—he'd made references to it while they dated, but it hadn't mattered to her, so she'd never cared beyond that. Then she remembered their conversation the evening of Hannah's recital. Her eyes widened. So he'd meant it that day!

"You didn't know?" Billy let out a sardonic laugh. "This is too funny. He's one of the richest men in the country. I guess he hid that from you." He pressed the knife in a little harder. "Now you're going to help me get some of that money. I'm going to ruin him for even trying to mess with me. I'm sure he'll give anything to save you. Not that you're even worth it. We'll go somewhere where it will just be you and me. I'll punish you for killing my brother, and then I'll send your broken pieces to him once he's handed over his money. By the time he receives you, I'll be long gone."

Emily's heart rate accelerated. Her worst nightmare had just come true. Billy might hurt Geoffrey, and it would be all her fault. She should have just stayed upstairs like Geoffrey had asked her to. She didn't care about how much money he had. She would rather die than help Billy ruin Geoffrey. This was one monster she would face alone.

"You always thought you were too good for

anyone," Billy continued. "That was why we chose you, and why Calvin met you that day at the convenience store. We'd laughed about it and decided we would get you no matter what it took. We would break you and turn you into a whore. And we were right. You were almost ready for me after he was done with you, and then you had to go get pregnant again. After all he had done to make sure you never had his baby. A baby would give you joy and purpose, and we didn't want that. You were our plaything after all. All he wanted was to get rid of the baby, but then you wrecked everything by killing him."

Emily's breath hitched, and anger began to grow at the bottom of her belly. She hadn't known it was their plan all along. Even though she'd found out after they got married that Calvin hadn't loved her, she'd never imagined that it was just a game to both of them. She'd always blamed herself for making the wrong choice in marrying her ex and for staying day after day after he'd started hitting her.

He kicked her on the leg. "Let's go."

Emily almost tumbled, and she righted herself in time. They'd stolen her life once, but she wasn't going to allow it again. "No, I'm not going anywhere with you," she said.

Billy pressed the knife harder against her neck and nicked the skin. She could feel the blood trickling down …

Emily's heart thudded against her chest, but she gritted her teeth in determination. Billy could kill her if he wanted, but she was no longer going to be afraid of him. She would stand her ground even if it meant certain death.

"You heard the lady. Let her go," a cold hard voice said.

A flicker of hope swelled in her chest. It wasn't a voice she knew, but it didn't matter. He was against Billy, which meant he was on her side.

The knife dug deeper into her neck at the man's voice. Billy wasn't going down without a fight.

Emily heard the unmistakable click of a gun. "I said let her go," the man repeated.

What happened next was a flurry of movement that felt like a dream. All Emily saw was Billy on the ground in handcuffs with a large man over him, the area flooded with lights, and other men she couldn't identify moving around.

Her knees grew weak, and she buckled.

But warm arms caught her. "I've got you." Geoffrey's familiar fresh scent tingled in her nose, and Emily knew she was safe.

Then she blacked out.

$\mathcal{E}$mily opened her eyes and looked around. She was in her bed at home. Had it all been a dream?

She touched her neck and noted the bandage over it. So it had really happened. But how had she ended up here?

That was when she noticed his head resting on the side of the bed, his eyes closed. Geoffrey. She reached out and ran her hand through his soft brown hair.

His eyes opened, and he sat up. "Are you feeling better?" he asked, concern written all over his face. She nodded. "Thank goodness," he said, reaching for her hand. "You scared me. I was so worried till the doctor assured me you were sleeping and would wake up soon."

"What happened?" she asked.

"Billy is in custody. When the warrant went out for his arrest, I had a feeling he might come to look for you, so I had some men stationed here, hidden in the shadows. I got the call as soon as he was sighted, but by the time I arrived, he'd already been taken down. We needed his confession, so my men waited till they had the evidence. I'm so sorry. But we got him good this time, and with what they have for all his other crimes, he won't be coming out for a very long time."

She loved this man. He was strong, beautiful, kind, and she didn't deserve him. But God had given her another chance, and she couldn't imagine staying one extra moment away from him—she'd realized how precious time was.

"I love you, Geoffrey Hart," she said.

"Are you okay, Emily?"

He still didn't get it. "And, yes, I will marry you."

She watched understanding dawn in his eyes. Geoffrey leaned forward and swept her into his arms.

"Ouch!"

Geoffrey loosened his hold. "I'm sorry, are you okay?"

She chuckled. "Just kidding."

"Really?"

"Well, it hurts a little."

He let go of her and brushed her hair behind her ear. "Thank you," he said.

"For?"

"For saying yes."

"I'm sorry for hurting you," Emily said. "I didn't want you involved in my mess."

"Emily, your life is not a mess. You're the most beautiful, courageous, and wonderful person I've ever met. You've gone through hell, yet you've come out strong."

"I'm not really that strong."

"Yes, you are." Geoffrey cupped the side of her face with his hand. "You're worth everything and more, and I'm honored to be able to spend the rest of my life with you."

Tears stung the back of Emily's eyelids. This man had no idea how much he meant to her. He was everything wonderful wrapped up in one gift and had shown her what it meant to have true love in her life.

"I love you, Geoffrey Hart," she said as a tear escaped and slid down her face.

Geoffrey leaned forward and kissed the tear away. His gorgeous brown eyes were shining, full of love and hope.

Her heart swelled with love, and all Emily wanted to do in that moment was to kiss him thoroughly, and so she did.

Emily kissed his forehead, an act that made his breath hitch and his eyes close in anticipation. She adored everything about this man who loved her with every fibre of his being. She kissed his eyes that saw the real her that needed to be loved and cherished. Then she pressed her lips lightly against his at first, giving him the sweet savor of love, joy, and longing that poured from her heart to his. Her heart rate quickened as his clean fresh scent wrapped itself around her and drew her close.

Emily's breath hitched as Geoffrey brushed his fingers against her cheek. He understood. This precious man understood what her heart was saying. He deepened the kiss, running his hands through her hair, giving her everything in return.

Geoffrey eventually broke the kiss and held her close, his arms holding her like she was the most precious thing in the world.

And in that moment, Emily believed it.

CHAPTER 39

*E*mily adjusted her sweater as she waited for Geoffrey to join her after parking the car in front of Dexington House. She'd been surprised to receive an invitation from Mrs. Dexington to spend Christmas Eve with them. She hoped Mrs. Dexington liked the bouquet of flowers she'd brought along.

"Are you ready?" Geoffrey asked as he looped his arm around her back. His touch calmed her racing heart, and Emily turned and smiled at him.

"As ready as can be."

"Don't worry she doesn't bite."

"I know. I've met her multiple times at

church and also at Phillip's wedding. But it's different being in her home."

"It's going to be fine, and Sarah is here as well."

Emily took a deep breath. "I'm ready." She hoped she looked okay in her red sweater and blue jeans. Mrs. Dexington had insisted they dress casual for the occasion.

Geoffrey opened the front door and led Emily through the cavernous foyer into the living room. He helped Emily take off her coat, which he hung in a coat room off the foyer.

Emily had to stop her jaw from dropping. The room gave off a Christmas candy land vibe without going over the top. A massive Christmas tree that twinkled with lights, glowing golden bells, and sparkling ornaments stood next to an intricately-designed fire place, and large presents already held their place under it. Emily could see Geoffrey had placed her presents there as well and was pleased they looked at home with the others.

"Welcome." Emily saw Helen Dexington hurrying toward her. She soon reached her and gave Emily a hug. "It's so good to see you again, Emily. Welcome to the family."

"Thank you, Mrs. Dexington. Here are some flowers for you." Emily handed her the bouquet.

Helen held the flowers against her nose. "They are lovely, thank you. Please call me Helen." By now, Helen's husband had joined them.

"Hello Emily," he said. "You can call me, Alex."

"Thank you, sir … I mean Alex."

"Oh, Alex, let the young lady relax," Helen scolded him.

"I didn't do anything." Alex raised his hands in mock defense.

Helen looped a hand around Emily's waist. "Come on, dear. It's time for dinner, and I'm sure you're hungry." She led them toward a massive table piled high with an assortment of holiday food.

"What about Phillip?" Geoffrey asked.

"He'll be down soon. Sarah needed a nap earlier, so he went to get her."

"Hi, Emily," a lovely voice said.

Emily turned to see an obviously-pregnant beautiful blonde smiling as she came down the stairs, led by Phillip.

"Hello, Sarah," Emily said with a smile in

return.

"Are you feeling better, dear?" Helen asked Sarah.

Sarah grinned. "Yes. But I'm so over this pregnancy, and I still have some months to go." She turned to Phillip. "It's all your fault."

"I'm sorry," Phillip said.

Everyone burst out laughing, which made Emily relax. She liked the fact they didn't take themselves too seriously, which was so unlike what she'd expected from such a distinguished family.

"Now let's eat," Helen said.

Dinner was a wonderful affair filled with so much joy and laughter that Emily felt like she fit right in. She saw a more relaxed side of Geoffrey than she'd ever seen before, and she especially loved the feel of his hand as he held hers under the table.

It reminded her of how her family dinner had been before her father passed on, and tears stung at the back of her eyes. Geoffrey gave her hand a reassuring squeeze like he understood, and Emily's heart filled with gratitude at his touch.

When dinner was over, Emily offered to clear the table. But she was surprised when everyone helped, and soon the dishes were cleared, washed, and left to dry.

"It's time," Helen said, when they were back in the living room. "Everyone, grab your coats."

"Where are we going?" Emily asked Geoffrey in a whisper.

"You'll see," he said with a cryptic smile. He grabbed Emily's coat plus a muffler and a hat. "You'll need these," he said as he helped her put on her coat.

So they were definitely spending some time outside.

But what could it be?

Emily couldn't believe what her eyes were seeing. Tractors with attached hayride wagons stood in rows in an open sports field not far from the local church and were already filled with people from the community.

"Yes, we are going Christmas caroling in

these hay wagons," Geoffrey confirmed. "Janet Jolley made all the arrangements."

Who would have thought? Emily didn't remember the last time she'd been part of a hay ride, and this looked like it was going to be so much fun.

Geoffrey led their little group to the one wagon that appeared empty. Small bales of hay lined the interior sides of the wagon and served as seats. Geoffrey and Phillip helped everyone else in their group into the wagon.

Fifteen minutes later, their procession began to move from the field with everyone singing "Joy to the World." If Emily had any doubts earlier, it was confirmed that Geoffrey was tone deaf, but she had to give him props for unabashedly belting out the song with all his heart.

They headed to the first nursing home where they sang more songs in the parking lot in front of the home. Then they moved to a nearby retirement home where the residents were already seated outside waiting for them.

The procession then made its way to the Dexington Medical Center before finally returning to the field where a crowd waited.

Any passersby would have assumed a game or concert was going on with how occupied the bleachers were. It turned into a Christmas carol celebration with the crowd singing along and waving their hands, and eventually ended with the local church's children's choir singing a beautiful rendition of "Silent Night."

A hush fell over the crowd as their voices soared in the air. Geoffrey put his arm around Emily and drew her close as they listened. Even Nancy had been able to locate her in the crowd, and it was a nice change to see Perry out and about.

This had been the best Christmas Eve ever. It was the greatest feeling in the world to be surrounded by her new family and a community she'd grown to love. And it had mostly happened because of the wonderful man standing next to her.

"Merry Christmas, Geoffrey Hart," she whispered to him.

Geoffrey drew her closer. "Merry Christmas to the most beautiful bride-to-be in the world." Then he fell on one knee and held a black box out to her. In it twinkled the most gorgeous diamond ring she'd ever seen. "Emily Roth, the most beautiful woman in the world and the owner of my heart, would you do me the honor of spending the rest of my life with me?"

The crowd around them went silent and waited for Emily to respond.

But Emily only had eyes for the man in front of her who had won her heart. "Yes. Yes!" she shouted.

Geoffrey slipped the ring on her finger to catcalls and clapping. Then he swept her into his arms and gave her a kiss in the true Geoffrey Hart fashion that she felt all the way to her toes.

It was indeed the perfect Christmas night ever.

"We're almost there," the midwife encouraged. "Just one more push. Take a deep breath and give it all you've got."

"You can do it," Geoffrey encouraged and swept Emily's sweat-soaked tendrils away from her face.

"Geoffrey Hart?" Emily said through gritted teeth.

"Yes, dear?"

"I'm going to kill you. Aaaah!"

Emily had dreaded it after her previous miscarriages, but she'd gotten pregnant anyway. The experience through it all had been night and day. Geoffrey had practically waited on her hand and foot, and she'd been pampered all the way.

Now she faced the kind of pain that reminded her too much of the miscarriages. But this time was different, because she would get to meet her rainbow baby.

Emily gripped Geoffrey's hand and gave the push all she could, though her insides felt like they were tearing apart. Geoffrey didn't even flinch, though she was pretty sure she'd almost crushed his hand. Good man.

"Yes, I can see his head now," the midwife said. "He's coming out. Keep going, mama."

But her body was tired and exhausted, and Emily didn't think she had the strength in her to continue.

"You can do this, Mila," Geoffrey said. This was his new nickname for her, the name he called her in the privacy of their bedroom when he showered her with kisses. "I know you're exhausted, but you're the strongest woman I know in the world."

He knew just what to say to her. Yes, she could do this. Just one more push. Emily grabbed her ankles with quivering hands and bore down. It was truly the end of the world like they had described it would be, and she was practically seeing stars.

Then she felt a release as something slipped out of her, and a baby's cry pierced the air.

Emily collapsed on the bed. She had done it! She turned to look at Geoffrey and noticed he had tears in his eyes. He leaned forward and kissed her forehead. "I love you," he whispered close to her ear.

She gave him a tired smile. "You were scared, right?"

"The whole time," Geoffrey responded. She liked that he could be vulnerable with her. It didn't make him less a man.

"Thank you for not showing it." She gave him a light kiss on the lips.

"Here you are," the midwife said handing over the red-faced baby with curly dark hair to Emily. "A beautiful baby boy."

Emily looked down at this boy she loved so much already even though they'd just officially met. She laid him against her breast, and soon he was rooting for it till he found it and latched onto it.

"He sure knows what he wants," Geoffrey

said, chuckling as he touched his baby's little toes.

Emily smiled. "Just like his daddy." They watched the baby as he suckled and then eventually fell asleep.

But there was someone else that was missing for their family to be complete, and Geoffrey understood.

"I'll go bring her," Geoffrey said. "I'm sure she's eager to meet her little brother."

Emily nodded. The midwives had finished cleaning her up so she could see visitors now.

Geoffrey kissed both her and the baby on the forehead and stepped out of the room.

"Mommy!" Emily looked up to see Hannah fly through the room a few minutes later. "A baby," she said with wonder in her voice. Geoffrey and Emily had adopted Hannah after they got married.

"Yes, your brother is finally here." Emily patted the space beside her in the bed, and Geoffrey lifted Hannah into it. Emily placed her other arm around Hannah and snuggled her close. "I've missed you," she said and kissed Hannah's head. Now she had her little family around her.

"The whole Dexington clan is here, but Helen insisted that everyone wait till you've had a chance to take a nap," Geoffrey said.

Emily smiled. Trust Helen to make sure everyone stayed in line. She'd become like a mom to her.

Emily could feel her eyes fluttering close. She was exhausted, but it had been worth it. Her heart was full, she had a new family who loved her, her precious kids, and a wonderful man at her side.

Her very own Billionaire Butler.

Thank you so much for reading! Want to know what happens next in Dexington, and how Veronica, Sarah's friend, finds love (an enemies-to-lovers romance)?

Check out A BILLIONAIRE DENTIST FOR CHRISTMAS at https://dobidaniels.com.

Here's an excerpt:

Something heavy crashed into Veronica. Her eyes flew open, and her arms flailed in an effort to find support. But there was nothing to grab onto, and she landed on her backside on the cobblestone.

Ouch! Veronica hoped her tailbone was not broken. What just…?

Her eyes widened in shock as a large slobbering tongue began to lick her face. The most beautiful dog she had ever seen, with a silver-grey coat and warm blue eyes, was lapping up her face like she was the most delicious ice cream he'd ever tasted. She couldn't help the laughter that bubbled up from her throat. Veronica had always wanted a dog, but she hadn't expected to become a treat for one.

"King, get off her!" a deep masculine voice commanded.

King? For goodness sake, who named their dog King?

The dog whined but obeyed, and then the dog owner came into view.

Well, well, well. If the dog was King, what would she call the owner that looked so delectable she could just stare at him all day? The beautiful—yes, beautiful instead of handsome—man standing in front of her looked at her with concern oozing from his warm brown eyes. Tall with his hair cut longer at the top and tapered on the sides, he wore a short well-groomed beard that finished off his polished masculine look.

The real-life Adonis extended a hand to her. "I'm so sorry about the dog. Let me help you up."

Her eyes couldn't help glancing at his ring finger. No ring. But that didn't mean he wasn't married—types like him never stayed long on the single market.

Veronica accepted his hand but almost let go from the immediate electric sparks that shot through her arm at their touch.

Hello! What was that? This man was supposed to be a total stranger. She had no business feeling this way with him.

"Are you okay?" he asked, oblivious to the thoughts that were running through her mind.

Her eyes darted to his lips as he spoke, and she almost melted. Veronica had never seen such kissable lips on a guy before. Gosh, he was really beautiful...

Want to read more? You can grab A BILLIONAIRE DENTIST FOR CHRISTMAS at https://dobidaniels.com!

Or want to know what happens next in Dexington?
Sign up now at https://dobidaniels.com.

If you've loved reading A Billionaire Butler for Christmas, Dobi would be grateful if you could spend a few minutes to leave a review (as short as you like) on the book's page on your favorite retailer. Your review would help bring it to the attention of other readers. Thank you very much.

Check out all Dobi Daniels books at https://dobidaniels.com

ACKNOWLEDGMENTS

Writing a book is harder and more rewarding than I could have ever imagined. And it would not have been possible without the support, love, and encouragement from my number one cheerleader, my dearest mom. My life would never have been this awesome and wonderful without you.

Of course, I have to thank my precious little DC for his smiles and antics. You brighten my day and give me the strength to keep pushing through.

Thank you to my sisters for encouraging me on this wonderful journey. And a special thanks to my baby brother (who is so not a baby anymore) for being super supportive and checking in on my progress. You guys are the best.

Thank you to my wonderful author friends. You know who you are. Your selflessness and willingness to share what you know has made my writing journey smoother and an exciting one. And a special thanks to Lisa and Deanna whose support have made a difference.

Most of all, I want to thank God who gave me life, surrounded me with the most wonderful people, and loved me all the way. You make my life complete.

And finally, a special thanks to all my readers whose love of my stories spur me on to write more. Thank you!

As a former physician and business executive in another life—with a childhood filled with reading multi-genre novels—Dobi Daniels loves to write sweet thrilling romance stories with heart. She enjoys dreaming up everyday characters who rise above unfavorable circumstances to overcome incredible odds and find joy along the way.

When not writing, Dobi can be found binging K-dramas and ice cream with her little sidekick by her side.

A Billionaire Butler for Christmas is the second book in the Dexington Christmas Billionaires Series. Sign up at dobidaniels.com to be notified when the next Dobi Daniels book comes out!

Thank you!

www.dobidaniels.com
hello@dobidaniels.com
facebook.com / dobidaniels
bookbub.com / profile / dobi-daniels
instagram.com / dobidaniels